Uncle Percy's Wonderful Town

Bruce Hutchison

Uncle Percy's Wonderful Town

Douglas & McIntyre/Vancouver

Copyright ©1981 by Bruce Hutchison

All rights reserved. No part of this book may
be reproduced or transmitted in any form by any
means without permission in writing from the
publisher, except by a reviewer, who may quote
brief passages in a review.

Douglas & McIntyre Ltd.
1615 Venables Street
Vancouver, British Columbia

Canadian Cataloguing in Publication Data.

Hutchison, Bruce, 1901-
  Uncle Percy's wonderful town

ISBN 0-88894-318-0

I. Title.

PS8515.U82U5   C813'.52   C81-091250-3
PR9199.3.H87U5

Line Drawings

Printed and bound in Canada by
The Bryant Press

Design: F.W. Hindle
Illustrations: William Taylor

To Hugh Kane, a great editor and faithful friend,
who knows books, language, life and other strange things.

Contents

Foreword

It was a lucky day for an old political reporter when he met two men rich in wisdom and experience, though perhaps too reckless in their trust. To both of them I owe my gratitude and admiration.

Without the help of Hugh Kane this book would not have been finished (nor anything of importance lost.) He had published my earlier book of factual recollections and read the beginnings of another manuscript altogether fictional. Only his strong encouragement and his offer to edit a text full of blemishes persuaded me to put down certain memories in form and style entirely different from my work of journalism.

Then luck was with me again. James Douglas, a bold and perceptive publisher, who had launched many better books, grasped at once what I was trying to say and agreed to set mine afloat.

It will surprise my friends, distressing some of them, because they have never heard, before now, about my youthful years in the dusty cow towns of British Columbia and expect a reporter to stick with reality.

They will guess, quite wrongly, that the town and characters herein recorded must be real, under slight disguise, when all of them are imagined, or at least far removed from the actual companions of those better days, long gone and by few remembered. But as Kane and Douglas understand, fiction is often truer than fact, more accurate than memory.

B.H. Victoria, B.C. April, 1981.

A Mighty Echo

The first telegram came at noon on May 5, 1910. I'm not likely to
forget that date. It was the eve of my fourteenth birthday.

Chief Skookum Barnabas of the Quintlam Reserve galloped
down the street from the railway station on his piebald mare and
left her untied by the hitching post. She was in a lather and so was
Barnabas. As he stumbled to the door of the print shop, his single
eye glaring, his row of silver teeth bared, I knew something must
be very wrong.

"For you, Percy," he said and dropped a yellow envelope on my
uncle's desk. "Bad news, eh?"

Everyone stopped to watch Uncle Percy. He tore the envelope
open and over his shoulder I read the typed words

KING DYING PREPARE SPECIAL EDITION WILL KEEP
YOU INFORMED.

The message from Vancouver was signed by Mike Brindle, publisher of the *Emerald Vale Weekly Echo*.

Uncle Percy's gold-rimmed glasses fell off his nose, leaving a red
spot on either side of it. His bony face turned pale and I thought he
was going to cry. But he only whispered to himself, "Loving God, I

can't believe it."

He had to believe it all the same. Brindle would be getting the news cabled from London to friends in the *Vancouver Gazette*.

Uncle Percy stared up at the colored picture on the wall above his desk. Edward VII was dressed in a fancy scarlet uniform with medals on his chest and a sword by his side. The sleepy eyes and wedge of black beard always frightened me a little but in our family the King was known to be the greatest of all living men. And now he was dying.

"I just can't believe it," Uncle Percy repeated, and suddenly he looked old, even older than his fifty-seven years. Then he seemed to recover. He rose to his full height, not much higher than my own, and ran his fingers through his mane of sandy hair and twirled his mustache into sharp points like copper wire.

I knew the signs. He was himself again. And I knew that Percival James Archer, my legal guardian, was unlike other men. He could do anything. I knew, too, that all his brains and experience were needed in this crisis.

The *Echo* had never published a special edition but every week it served nearly a thousand subscribers in our booming town of Emerald Vale and reached the outskirts of Kamloops and Ashcroft. On its masthead it claimed to be "The Voice of British Columbia's Last Green Frontier". No one disputed the claim even if the frontier was brown and dusty most of the time.

Only because of his close friendship with Mike Brindle, Uncle Percy had neglected his real estate business and his duties as Justice of the Peace to edit the *Echo* for a couple of weeks. He loved journalism after his training in Fleet Street, his education at Oxford and his years of fighting in the South African War but he was not a man to boast of his great career. I felt sure he would turn out a memorial worthy of the King.

Now he thrust his personal feelings aside and shouted to the foreman, "Stop the press!"

Alf Gropp was printing the monthly handbills that I would deliver for Grimshaw's Central Emporium and they fluttered off

12

the press in a pink stream. The press clanked and trembled but it stopped. Gropp came grumbling to Uncle Percy's desk—a tiny man just a year out of England. His shriveled face made me think of a stale lemon.

"Wot in 'ell's the trouble?"

Uncle Percy showed him the telegram.

Gropp pushed his greasy wig to the side of his glistening head.

"Dyin' is 'e, the poor old barstard? No wonder, after all 'is carry on."

Uncle Percy looked furious but he spoke quietly, as always.

"Edward is a great King. A man among men."

"Yus, and wimmin, too. Heh, heh."

Gropp's cackle sounded like our green parrot but Uncle Percy ignored it.

"We'll run six pages tomorrow," he said.

"Six bloody pages? And not a line set! Christ, and 'im not dead yet. Wot if he don't? Oh, 'e's tough, that one."

"We must be ready for the worst. And we'll hold the paper till we know, of course. Six full pages, mind. Fill them out with pictures. And strip the ads off the front."

"Wot! Strip the ads, and them under contrack? Brindle won't like it."

"No matter, strip them."

This, I knew, was a drastic move. The *Echo* earned $10 a week from the largest ad in the upper right hand corner of the front page. It recommended Dr. Jonathan Tuttle's Magic Formula, a laxative "as gentle as an April zephyr" and asked the reader, "Why Blast Your Bowels with Nauseous Remedies?" In the opposite corner a second ad for The Original Virginia Potion guaranteed a cure for Lost Manhood.

Even lost revenue couldn't deter Uncle Percy.

"Strip them," he said again.

Gropp flung out his arm at the *Echo*'s antique machinery.

"Fill six pages! Wif this lot of rubbish? You're mad. Why, it'll take all night."

"No doubt. But we did it in Fleet Street. We can do it here."

"Not wif me you can't. Work like a 'orse, treated like a dog, I'm orf."

The same threat was made every second day but Gropp went back to the type boxes, muttering.

Under all the strain Uncle Percy stayed calm. He took off his coat, hung it on a peg, arranged his detachable starched cuffs neatly on the desk and filled his fountain pen from a rubber syringe to write the royal obituary.

When Paul Jessup, the *Echo*'s reporter, arrived from the monthly beef auction on the only bicycle in Emerald Vale I told him the news. His fishy eyes popped behind his thick spectacles and his narrow, bloodless face began to twitch.

"If the King is dying," he said, "it's serious."

With Jessup everything was serious and his knowledge was immense. He had graduated from Toronto University, worked for the *Globe* and resigned in a dispute on editorial policy. Or so he often explained.

Uncle Percy doubted his story and regarded Jessup as a radical, most likely a socialist. They seldom spoke to each other and then they always ended in a shouting match. But this was no time for shouting.

Jessup hurried to Uncle Percy's desk.

"Mr. Archer, I understand you intend to publish a special edition. Really, sir, it would be premature, a serious mistake..."

Uncle Percy's voice was quiet but firm.

"Mr. Jessup, that's for me to decide. We publish."

Jessup spluttered and waved his hands.

"It's premature, unethical, irresponsible. However..."

He pulled a notebook from his pocket and held it close to his spectacles.

"The beef auction," he said, "should be worth a column. Prices high, extraordinary. Five cents on the hoof. One bull, Hereford, sold for three hundred dollars. And a milking shorthorn from the Douglas Lake herd, twelve quarts a day, and as fine a pair of tits as it was ever my pleasure to handle..."

Uncle Percy gaped up at him.

"Milking shorthorns! Fine tits! Mr. Jessup, have you taken leave of your senses? The King is dying."

"Yes, sir, possibly. Even so, the local news should run. Ranchers depend..."

The fountain pen dropped from Uncle Percy's hand.

"Ranchers be damned! Not a line on cattle, Mr. Jessup. If you wish to help me go and sort out the cuts. We'll need pictures to save setting. And fillers, a dozen at least."

Jessup frequently resigned on issues of editorial policy and now, as he stood twitching before Uncle Percy, I thought he would resign again. Then he seemed to change his mind.

"Cuts and fillers? Very good, Mr. Archer."

I saw that he expected the special edition to be unworthy of the *Echo* without the local news but after a moment he sat down at his own desk and started to pound the only typewriter in the office.

Jessup took pride in his short paragraphs that filled the blank spaces at the bottom of the columns. He spent hours studying the *Encyclopedia Britannica,* the *Dictionary of Natural Phenomena* and other reference works. Most of the resulting fillers were historical and biological. The *Echo*'s readers learned a lot from Jessup.

A recent issue had informed them that William the Conqueror's birth was out of wedlock, that Cleopatra was of Negro origin and that the Great Horned Owl of Alaska swallowed mice whole, regurgitating the bones at leisure. Jessup had once reported that "Karl Marx first exposed the evils of Capitalism," and Brindle had fired him on the spot. He was rehired next day because his factual notes gave the *Echo* certain tone, Brindle said, and the readers seemed to enjoy them.

As Jessup pulled the first page from his typewriter Uncle Percy beckoned to me.

"David," he whispered, "watch what that man writes. I know his tricks. A dangerous, treacherous sneaky fellow, a fat-faced pedant and a republican too, I shouldn't wonder. Watch him. But wait. I

15

must wire Brindle."

He scribbled a telegram.

SPECIAL EDITION WELL IN HAND STOP SIX PAGES FIT-
TING TRAGIC OCCASION AND PRESS WILL ROLL MID-
NIGHT STOP ADVISE ME LATEST DEVELOPMENTS.

This was not quite accurate since the flat-bed press had no
rollers but Brindle would understand.

Uncle Percy handed me the message.

"Wait for a reply. And, David, hurry."

I forgot all about Jessup's fillers and dashed out the back door
and jumped on Dock, my roan cayuse, without bothering to saddle
him. He moved off, snorting, at a walk but I dug my heels into his
flanks and he broke into a gallop down the street, across the bridge
to the station.

Lem Brady, the railway agent, was dozing beside his telegraph
key, a green shade over his eyes and a wet cigarette dangling from
his lips. I nudged him awake and he read the telegram.

"Okay kid," he said, "but Percy's sure takin' chances. There's no
more news from Vancouver."

He wiped his pasty face with a red bandana and fingered the
key. I waited for the reply outside in the shade of the porch. The key
chattered for a minute or two and then silence. Lem dozed off.

It was a full hour before I heard the key again and the rattle of
Lem's typewriter. He came to the door and handed me a yellow
paper.

"Better get that to Percy quick. The boss is all shook up."
Brindle's telegram shook me up, too.

HOLD EVERYTHING STOP PATIENT MUCH IMPROVED
STOP AWAIT INSTRUCTIONS STOP ARE YOU CRAZY.

I stuck the paper in my pocket and swung up to the saddle. As
Dock galloped past her house the good-looking woman known
only as Miss Stella yelled at me from the window. I kept going and
yelled back, "patient much improved."

16

Dandy Ryan was standing with some cowboys in front of his Majestic Hotel and they tried to stop me but I yelled again, "patient much improved" and lashed Dock with my quirt.

When I got to the office Uncle Percy was writing fast. His white collar lay on the desk beside a tumbler of water. Or it might have been gin.

He read the telegram and flung it into the waste basket.

"Wot's that about?" Gropp snarled across the shop.

"It's nothing," said Uncle Percy. "Brindle's lost his head, that's all. As if we'd print before we knew. Ridiculous. Steady, boys. Get on with it."

He settled down to work again but I saw that the obituary wasn't going well. Already the waste basket overflowed with discarded opening paragraphs and I read them when he wasn't looking.

In one he had written that, "The glorious pageant of England's history produced few men who..." in another that "The spirit immortal of the British race lives on..." and in another that "A world hushed in sorrow sheds honorable tears for a King of modest majesty who..."

None of these opening paragraphs satisfied Uncle Percy but at last he had got under way with some lines from Tennyson that I remembered from my school reader.

> Not once or twice in our rough island story
> The path of duty was the way to glory.

Below the quotation his pen moved in a jerky scrawl. He sipped from the glass and murmured to himself.

"Lord save the virgin's precious flesh!" he cried aloud. Then, after a pause, "to your tents, oh Israel" and "washed in the blood of the lamb." The words made no sense to me but I guessed they were out of the Bible. He was a very religious man.

When he had filled each sheet I took it to the printers. Gropp was dismantling the type set for next week's regular edition. His hands, black with ink, moved like two hungry sparrows as he lifted the metal letters and tossed them into their narrow boxes. His

Swedish assistant, Rolf Erickson, had come late, an unlighted cigar thrust into his golden beard and a mickey in his hip pocket.

"Skoal!" he said and took a long swig from the bottle.

He offered it to Gropp who drank deep.

"Bloody Canajian rye but not bad," he grunted and laid his wig on the shelf above the type boxes. Four grimy sparrows kept pecking. Rolf slowly ate his cigar but never spat out any juice. I always wondered how he could do it.

Jessup was still pounding his typewriter and after he had written a couple of fillers he would hang them on the printers' spike. Nobody had time to read them.

Gropp had just started to set the obituary when Skookum Barnabas brought the third telegram from Brindle and gave it to Uncle Percy.

SINKING FAST BUT DO NOT REPEAT NOT PRINT BEFORE MY ARRIVAL TOMORROW TRAIN

"No answer," Uncle Percy told Barnabas and threw the telegram on the floor. "Poor Brindle, he's getting hysterical. Does he imagine that I'd...oh well."

The obituary was going fine and must have reached a thousand words by this time but it had taken a lot out of Uncle Percy. His reddish hair hung damp on his forehead. The copper points of his mustache had wilted. The tumbler was empty.

Darkness had come outside but the sizzling acetylene lamps kept the shop bright. Their fumes mixed with the smell of ink, metal and oil. Gropp and Erickson had finished off their bottle and swayed on their feet but their hands pecked steadily at the boxes of letters. New type was spreading across the stone inside the six steel chases.

The printers seemed to have a private joke between themselves. I couldn't tell what they were chuckling about as they set Jessup's fillers. But I heard them arguing over an old proof of the editorial that Brindle had written in his best style for the next regular edition and they decided to hold it in type. It was headed "What now, Gutless Wonder?" That, of course, would be the *Echo*'s latest comment on Sir Wilfrid Laurier.

"Bloody good stuff," said Gropp. "Brindle can use it any time. Laurier ain't dead yet."

"Yah, too bad," Erickson giggled.

"An' we'll keep the medicine ads in. Never mind old Percy. It's them as pays the wages."

"Yah, but what about the fillers?"

"Stick 'em in, fill 'er up. Doesn't matter. Brindle won't let the bloody paper out anyways."

They kept setting type and laying it on the stone.

Uncle Percy was still writing, but slowly, and the pen shook in his hand.

Jessup had finished his copy and I helped him arrange the cuts on a dummy sheet. We couldn't find many in the cupboard to choose from. The only picture of the King was a rough line drawing that showed him as Prince of Wales at a race track in a top hat.

"It'll do for the last King of England," said Jessup.

The cut of Edward's son, George, the next King, I supposed, was in half-tone from a photo taken when he'd been a midshipman with a telescope at his eye. There were no cuts of Queen Alexandra and her other children.

"We'll use Victoria instead," said Jessup. "She fits in anywhere. It doesn't matter. All a farce, the Empire, the raj, dominion over palm and pine—bah!"

I thought the old Queen looked pretty good under her crown and she filled a lot of space. So did Kitchener and Asquith, though I'd never heard of them before. We still had an empty page and chose a four-column cut of Buckingham Palace and another of Piccadilly Circus and a large view of Westminster Abbey.

Jessup decided to use Laurier as well but when we showed the cut to Uncle Percy he exploded.

"That damned Liberal? No, no. The man's not loyal. And French!"

"He's Prime Minister," Jessup protested. "Surely, sir, we can't leave him out on grounds of politics? A serious omission..."

"You may be right," Uncle Percy admitted. "If we must we must. But don't leave Borden out either. He's loyal."

We found a smudged cut of Sir Robert Borden at the back of the cupboard.

Uncle Percy finished the obituary just after two o'clock in the morning.

"A bit knocked up, David," he said and handed me the final page. "Now for a little nap. I find there's nothing so restful as sleep."

He rubbed his eyes, picked up the tumbler but found it empty and slumped down in his chair.

I took the copy to Gropp. He and Erickson had used up a second mickey. Gropp's face was smeared with ink, his legs seemed weak and he sprawled over the chase, pawing the type, moving it around and trying to equalize the column with Jessup's fillers. But he stopped to squint at Uncle Percy's last paragraph.

"Cor! Wot's this? Royal throne of kings, other Eden, demi-paradise? And the bloke not dead yet! Percy's ravin' mad."

"Don't worry," Erickson grunted. "Brindle's goin' to kill it all."

He started to set the copy. His fingers were clumsy and some of the type dropped to the floor. He didn't bother to collect it.

I thought the printers must be getting drunk but was too tired to care and lay down on a pile of newsprint in the corner of the shop. It couldn't have been long before Aunt Minerva wakened me. She bustled into the office with a package of sandwiches and a thermos of coffee. That was like her. She had a big heart, big body and a rosy, laughing face.

But she wasn't laughing now. She was sniffing.

"My land! Liquor! Ha, I can smell it."

She tugged her husband's shoulder.

"Wake up; Percy! Wake up!"

He raised his head and tried to smile but didn't quite succeed.

"Percival Archer," she cried, "I believe you're intoxicated!"

"Not at all, my dear. Only tired. A hard day. The King is dying," he added in a shaky voice.

"That's as may be. But you're coming home."

She dragged him to his feet and started for the door. Uncle Percy turned back to us.

"Roll the press when it's ready. Lock up the papers till Brindle gets here. Guard them with your life..."

"Fiddlesticks," said Aunt Minerva and the door closed behind them.

I lay down again on the pile of newsprint. The clanking of the press roused me. Gropp was thrusting blank pages into it and they flew out faster than Erickson could stack them.

I'd just glanced at the black double headline, "The King is Dead, Long Live the King", flanked by the ads for mild laxative and restored manhood, when I heard the chug of the Reo outside. There was no mistaking the sound of Dandy Ryan's crimson automobile, the first one in town. Both cylinders snorted as loud as gunshots.

Dandy pushed through the door, nifty in his bowler hat and bulging flowered vest but his jowls were blotched and unshaved, his eyes wild.

Two other men followed him. I recognized Jake Hogarth, the lanky boss of the Circle Z, with his fringed buckskin coat and a face of the same stuff. Doc Foster, the vet from the livery stable, came last, his white billy goat's beard wagging.

Dandy lurched across the shop and as he passed me I caught the whiff of cigars and whisky from his Majestic Hotel.

"Let's see it!" he bawled. "Let's see the paper!"

Gropp stepped in front of the press.

"Nobody sees it till Brindle gets 'ere. Nobody."

"Oh yeah? Say, whoya think owns this goddamn shebang? Me, that's who. Hand it over".

He pushed Gropp aside and yanked a paper from the stack.

"Not yet," I managed to say.

Dandy paid no attention but stared at the front page obituary, his mouth open, the dark jowls quivering.

"What's this?" he burst out. "Not once or twice in our rough island story! For God's sake! Napoleon suffered acutely from hemorrhoids at the battle of Waterloo! What, what? Napoleon, hemorrhoids! Is this a joke or something?"

Hogarth was gaping at another column. "No joke. Get this—the noble pageant of England's history will not see his like again— oysters of the Atlantic Ocean reproduce themselves without sexual intercourse. Christ, that's a beaut!"

Doc Foster peered at the half-tone cuts.

"General Kitchener," he squeaked, "the Gutless Wonder! Socialism was born in the Sermon on the Mount..."

Dandy's jowls had turned as crimson as his Reo "Who done this?" he hollered. "Who done it?"

I knew in a flash who'd done it. Gropp had scattered Jessup's fillers all through the paper. Even a report of the beef auction, with an elegant description of the milking shorthorn's udder, took up a column on the back page, illustrated by Laurier's picture. But it was too late now to change anything.

Jessup huddled behind the press, wringing his soft hands.

"Please, gentlemen, please," he stammered. "The paper hasn't been released. Typographical errors soon corrected. It would be serious if..."

"Work like a 'orse, treated like a dog," said Gropp. "I'm orf."

He took his wig from the shelf and placed it carefully on his head. Then he sank slowly to the floor and began to blubber. Erickson grinned and chewed the stump of his wet cigar.

"Somebody'll pay for this!" Dandy bellowed. He pulled a big gold watch out of his vest pocket. "It's late. Train's due any minute. Where's Percy?"

"He went home," I whispered.

"Gone is he? By God, we'll fix him. Come on boys."

He grabbed an armful of papers and went howling through the door. Hogarth and Foster scurried after him with more papers.

"A serious business," said Jessup but I thought he was smiling.

I jumped on Dock just as daylight was breaking. By the time I got to the station the Reo was there already. Dandy stood on the platform, Uncle Percy beside him, shivering in a green bathrobe over his pyjamas and blinking, half blind, without his glasses. A dozen other men clustered around, each of them holding a copy of the paper. The train puffed across the bridge.

Through the office window I saw Lem Brady leaning over the ticker but it was silent. The wire to Vancouver hadn't opened yet.

The train pulled in. Before it stopped Brindle stepped down to the platform looking, as he always did, like Humpty Dumpty. He wore a brand new checked suit too tight for his swollen belly and a white Panama hat and a scowl on his ivory face.

Dandy rushed at him, waving the paper.

"See what they done! And him not even dead yet!"

Brindle gawked at the *Echo's* front page and his three chins throbbed. Very slowly, he tore the paper into neat ribbons and threw them under the train. The steam blew them away.

I expected the usual hysterics of his editorials but the words came out softly as if he were praying.

"Ruined. Betrayed. Bitched. A laughing stock. A holy show."

"I gave strict orders," Uncle Percy began but Brindle cut him short.

"Forget it. My own fault for leavin' the paper with a lunatic. And an Englishman at that."

Suddenly, from the back of the crowd, I heard the ticker start in the office and saw Lem scribbling on a yellow pad. Now he came running and whooping to the platform.

"He's gone! The King's gone!"

"Eh? Eh?" Dandy gasped. "You got it straight?"

"Straight from London to Vancouver. Dead all right, ten minutes ago."

Brindle was the first to recover. He took off the Panama and pressed it to his chest.

"The King," he said. "God rest him."

Dandy hesitated but took off his bowler, too, and all the men stood for a moment bareheaded.

Then Brindle clutched Uncle Percy's hand and slapped him on

the shoulder.

"You did it, old pal, you did it! Scooped the world. A clean beat."

"All in the day's work," Uncle Percy gulped.

"No, sir, no!" And in his best writing style Brindle uttered a phrase I'll never forget. "Friends, neighbors and citizens of Emerald Vale, thanks to Percy Archer, that great man of letters, the *Echo* resounds from one end of the country to the other! Yes, sir, a Mighty Echo!"

"You betcha!" cried Dandy. "And this calls fer a drink. On the house. Let's go!"

"In the circumstances," Uncle Percy muttered, "I hardly think..."

But Dandy hustled him and Brindle into the Reo and it sputtered off to the Majestic.

I was mounting Dock when Jessup pedalled down the street on his bicycle and I told him what had happened. "It's a world scoop, a clean beat."

"Merely coincidence," said Jessup. "Sensational yellow journalism. A serious breach of ethics. I'll resign, of course."

His fishy eyes gazed at me through the thick spectacles.

"You realize what this means, boy? No more kings, the end of the monarchy. But that's not serious."

24

Sir John's Bed

I couldn't have chosen a worse time to set Sir John A. Macdonald's bed on fire when another great man was about to sleep in it—so great that Uncle Percy said he would be the next Prime Minister of Canada.

Aunt Minerva had warned me often enough to stay out of the upstairs room where my uncle slept alone in the famous bed and kept his *lares* and *penates,* as he called them. The words—Latin I understood—seemed to mean his books, papers, pictures and the gun and sword he carried in the South African war. His green parrot lived there, too, in a round cage, eating sunflower seeds and talking to himself. Uncle Percy had trained him in military language and named him General Brock in honor of the hero of Queenston Heights.

I sometimes sneaked into the room, of course, but only for a minute or two and no one had caught me, so far. The chance to take a leisurely look came on a Sunday morning.

Uncle Percy, Aunt Minerva and her old-maid sister, Lizzy, were at church and, because I had an essay to write for school on Monday—or said I had—they left me in the house with Marie, the French Canadian cook. She had the weekly chicken in the oven and was rolling out pastry for her regular Sunday pie, so she didn't see me climb the stairs and softly open the bedroom door.

The bed took up most of the room. It was made of dark oak with four tall posts and a headboard carved in a fancy design of leaves and acorns. Aunt Minerva's parents and my grandparents, the Crawleys, had brought it from England long ago to Ontario. They lived in a stone house beside the St. Lawrence and three times Sir John A., my grandfather's friend and idol, had visited the house and slept in the bed. Naturally, it was given his name and recognized as the most sacred of the *lares* and *penates*. To hear Aunt Lizzy talk, you'd have thought that Sir John was a member of the family but Aunt Minerva was less enthusiastic. She said he drank too much and had a whisky nose.

Uncle Percy had never seen Macdonald and didn't remember his wife's people, having married her on his own arrival in Canada from London. By that time all of them, including my mother, were dead, except for Minerva and Lizzy. But he revered the great man's memory and shipped his bed to British Columbia, along with the rest of the family furniture, when he built the first brick house, the only fireproof house, in Emerald Vale.

The bed was polished every month. Uncle Percy wouldn't allow anyone else to touch it and applied a special English paste himself. The care of old oak, he said, was a skill known only in England.

Above the bed he had hung an oil painting of Macdonald in a huge gilt frame and beside it a tinted photograph of Sir Richard McBride, the Conservative Premier of British Columbia. The photograph bore McBride's signature under the inscription, "To my good and cherished friend, Percy, with admiration, Dick."

Their friendship was so close that even Uncle Percy's defeat as the Conservative candidate for the provincial legislature at Victoria in two elections had not strained it in the least. And soon Sir Richard was coming to occupy Sir John's room and his bed.

These arrangements had caused some family dispute which I had managed to overhear by stealthy eavesdropping.

Everyone in the house worshipped Macdonald but Aunt

28

Minerva wasn't sure about McBride after she had once seen him in the bar of the Majestic Hotel drinking with Uncle Percy.

"He's a politician if you ask me," she sniffed.

"Ah, but he's still young," said Uncle Percy. "He'll grow. Dick's going to beat Laurier. Borden can never do it. Just wait a few years."

Aunt Minerva puffed out her fleshy pink cheeks.

"Your Dick! Why, he's not even a gentleman."

Aunt Lizzy jumped up with a tinkle of her glass beads.

"For shame!"

Her long horse face puckered and she whinnied like a horse, too.

"The idea! And don't forget that Sir John wasn't born a gentleman, either."

"Nor was our Lord," Uncle Percy murmured, "but nature's gentlemen, all of them."

"Twaddle!" said Aunt Minerva. "You and your politics."

"Now, now, my love. You're unreasonable. A touch of the Crawley."

Those were the strongest words he ever used against his wife and they always stung her. But in the end she agreed that Sir Richard could use Sir John's bed while Uncle Percy moved to a little room in the attic.

Now, as I stood on the bed and peered closely at the two portraits, Macdonald looked old and McBride young but they resembled each other almost, I thought, like father and son. Both had the same bulging forehead, the wrinkled eyes, the plumes of white curls around their high, starched collars. The pictures I had seen of Laurier in the newspapers showed a third man wreathed in curls and I supposed that all great men wore their hair like that as a kind of trademark.

There were many other fascinating things in the room.

General Brock croaked hoarsely in his cage hanging from a bracket. A small plaster bust of Sir John stood on the table, his personal gift to my Grandfather Crawley, but it didn't look much like the oil portrait. Below the sword and gun, a Zulu spear was fastened to the wall and its point felt sharp against my finger.

In the big oak wardrobe I found Uncle Percy's dress suit, a scarlet uniform with gold trimmings and a bottle of whisky hidden behind his neat row of boots. Best of all, on the mahogany desk, was a hollow elephant's foot, rimmed in silver, and full of tobacco beside a box of matches. That was the beginning of the trouble.

I took one of the pipes from the rack above the table and crammed some tobacco into it and struck a match. If the tobacco had burned I probably would have been sick at my stomach and no harm done. But it wouldn't burn. I struck several more matches without success and tossed them through the open window.

The tobacco was just starting to burn nicely at last when the lace curtains around the window exploded in one flash. I tried to pull them down before the fire could spread but they were too hot to touch. So I grabbed the Zulu spear and stabbed them. They fell in smoking pieces and the flames oozed across the carpet.

"Company halt!" General Brock croaked from his cage.

Dropping the spear, I remembered the bottle in the wardrobe and emptied it on the carpet. That didn't help. The flames rose higher and by now had reached the bed, crawling up the fringe of the quilt.

At this moment the fat, glistening figure of Marie waddled through the door. With acute presence of mind, she instantly grasped the situation.

"Fire!" she howled, "Mother of God, it *is* fire!"

Gabbling in French, she dragged me to the door. Before she closed it behind us I snatched up the parrot's cage. "Form fours," he said as we tumbled down the stairs.

In the kitchen Marie clutched me to her vast bosom and called me *"mon brave"* and *"pauvre blessé."* She seemed to think I had discovered the fire and tried heroically to put it out. I didn't correct her.

Just then the front door was opened by Uncle Percy in his top hat and frock coat, his mustache waxed to sharp Sunday points. He was followed by Aunt Minerva in a dress of rustling blue silk and a hat of feathers, and Aunt Lizzy in green silk and a hat of flowers.

Aunt Minerva twitched her blunt nose.

"I smell smoke!"

"So do I!" cried Aunt Lizzy.

"Nonsense, my dears," said Uncle Percy but then he dropped his cane and ran up the stairs three steps at a time.

Aunt Minerva swept into the kitchen.

"My land, Marie, what's happened?"

"Fire!" Marie groaned. "He tried to put it out but it wouldn't."

"Ha!" said Aunt Minerva. "I knew it. Percy smoking in bed again."

She rushed back to the hall where Aunt Lizzie stood with her mouth open watching Uncle Percy run downstairs. He carried Sir John's portrait outstretched in his hands as if it were hot.

"The house!" he yelled. "It's on fire!"

"Indeed?" said Aunt Minerva. "Well, don't just stand there. Call the fire department."

"In Sir John's room," Aunt Lizzy whimpered. "Oh, to think..."

Uncle Percy was at the telephone cranking the handle and shouting into the mouthpiece.

"Send the engine right away! Where? Here, you fools. And hurry."

He turned from the telephone and glared at Aunt Minerva.

"They'll be late. A pack of damned Grit heelers, the lot of them."

"Don't swear, Percy."

"And on Sunday, too," Aunt Lizzy whined.

"Loving Jesu!" said Uncle Percy and ran upstairs again. Smoke was pouring under the bedroom door.

Aunt Minerva took Sir John's portrait out to the front verandah.

Aunt Lizzy had collapsed on the hall bench with a handkerchief pressed to her nose.

"Stop sniveling," said Aunt Minerva. "Save the silver and china."

"What would Sir John say?" Aunt Lizzy sniveled but she tottered with me to the dining room and we began to carry the silver and plates out to the back yard. Some of the china wasn't broken.

Marie took the chicken and the pie from the oven and laid them carefully on the lawn. I put the parrot cage beside them.

"Steady, lads, steady," said General Brock.

Now I heard the bells and the volunteer fire department clattered up the street, six firemen clinging to the engine, four horses at the gallop.

Chief Ben Stott burst through the front door. He was in a big leather helmet and a long oil-skin coat over his stiff white Sunday shirt. His spiked beard looked very black, his face very red.

"What's goin' on here?" he demanded.

"The house is on fire," said Aunt Minerva. "You booby."

The Chief scratched his beard.

"I thought as much."

"Did you really? Clever fellow. Brilliant."

"Keep cool ma'am. Keep cool."

"Keep cool yourself and get the fire out."

"We'll get her out all right. Come on, boys, hose and axes."

It was wonderful, how this squat bear of a man could lead the fire department so confidently when I had seen him every day weighing meat in his butcher shop and joking with the customers.

He rammed the helmet further down on his head and leaped up the stairs, the firemen after him with axes and a hose, but he collided with Uncle Percy on the way down. One quick jab of the Chief's elbow thrust him aside and he staggered down the rest of the steps to the hall, his top hat rolling with him. When he reached the bottom I saw the bust of Sir John gripped in his arms.

The Chief swung an axe at the bedroom door without bothering to notice that it wasn't locked.

Uncle Percy examined the bust intently.

"Ruined! There's a piece broken off the nose."

"Get to work," said Aunt Minerva. "It was too long anyhow."

On her knees with a dish cloth she was wiping up the puddles from the hose.

The Chief appeared at the top of the stairs.

"It looks bad!" he panted. "Better take out the furniture."

"You take it out," Aunt Minerva shouted back and kept mopping the puddles. "That's what you're paid for."

"Never paid a cent. But it's your furniture. It'll burn good."

He came down the stairs, his white shirt front torn open, his chest naked and hairy.

"Oh, oh, oh," Aunt Lizzy whinnied. "What would Sir John say?"

"He'd say shut your mouth and get the hell out of the way," the Chief shouted and ran out the door to the fire engine.

"My God!" Uncle Percy gasped. "I forgot McBride!"

He lurched up the stairs and came down holding the photograph of Sir Richard and the gun from South Africa.

The Chief had just returned, carrying a long crowbar. When he saw the gun he backed into the doorway and raised the crowbar above his shoulder like a club.

"Don't shoot!"

Uncle Percy gave him a withering glance.

"You take me for crazy?"

"I do for a fact. Crazy as a coot."

He lowered the crowbar and mounted the stairs. Water poured from the ceiling and I heard the crash of axes. But there seemed to be less smoke.

Aunt Minerva and I were moving furniture out of the dining room when Uncle Percy charged in.

"Save the furniture!" he hollered.

"Pull yourself together and help us," said Aunt Minerva.

Aunt Lizzy groped in the sideboard for the linen. "To think of it," she sobbed.

Marie was mumbling in French as she gathered up the pots and pans.

Suddenly Uncle Percy remembered his parrot.

"Where's Brock?"

He dropped a chair and dashed out the kitchen door. General Brock was safe on the grass eating sunflower seeds.

"Good chap," said Uncle Percy. "Keep your pecker up."

"About turn," the parrot replied.

"Come and get to work," Aunt Minerva yelled through the doorway.

Together we struggled to move the sideboard and had just got it as far as the kitchen when the Chief stumbled down the stairs, his helmet missing, his oil-skin coat dripping.

"Well?" asked Aunt Minerva.

"We've put her out," he grunted.

"Took your time about it. And ruined the carpets."

The Chief stamped out the front door.

When the firemen had left on their engine we moved the furniture in again and Marie used the burned chicken to make some sandwiches. We ate them in silence at the kitchen table until Uncle Percy began to fidget.

"I wouldn't have believed it could happen," he grumbled. "Hours afterwards."

"Why not?" said Aunt Minerva. "It was smouldering in the mattress all the time we were at church."

"Impossible, my dear."

"But it happened. When the child opened the door the flames were all over the room. Thanks to you he nearly burned to death. And the house, too."

"Impossible. The house is fireproof. Brick."

"Poppycock! Nothing's safe when you smoke in bed. A vile habit."

"I never smoke in bed," said Uncle Percy.

Aunt Minerva shook her finger at him.

"Don't quibble. I told you and I told you and I told you but no, you wouldn't listen."

"A touch of the Crawley," Uncle Percy murmured.

"And remember, there'll be no smoking in this house as long as I'm here. Not in any room, mind."

Here was my moment of test and, of course, I failed it. When I opened my mouth to confess Aunt Minerva shushed me.

34

"Be quiet, child. It wasn't your fault. You saved us all."

At my age of fourteen I didn't like to be called a child but maybe it was better than being found out, I shut my mouth.

"What about the insurance?" Aunt Minerva demanded.

"Fully covered," said Uncle Percy. "House, furniture, everything."

"Nothing covers this mess. And your precious friend, McBride, due next month. Well, he won't smoke here I can tell you. And no drinking, either."

"As you say, my dear. But we'll be ready for Sir Richard."

"You'd better be. *Sir* Richard indeed! What's the country coming to!"

On Monday morning the carpenters started the repairs. New rugs and curtains were ordered from Vancouver, the rooms upstairs papered, Sir John's bed scraped and varnished.

His portrait and Sir Richard's photograph were touched up by Tim Morley, the house painter. He didn't claim to be a real artist but in his spare time he'd decorated the walls of his shop with some rare pictures of a harem, the Turkish ladies all fat and naked.

Uncle Percy wasn't quite satisfied with the work on Sir John.

"His nose couldn't have been that red," he grumbled.

All this time my conscience nagged me until I blurted out the truth to Aunt Minerva—the pipe, the tobacco, the matches.

She gave me a puzzled look that turned into a half smile.

"There, there, child," she said and wiped my tears on her apron. "You're a brave boy to take the blame but your uncle lighted it. No doubt of that."

Then, with a hard glint in her eye: "And don't ever tell him different. He's got to learn his lesson. He'll never smoke in this house again."

I promised not to tell Uncle Percy and of course I did the very next day when I found him sitting alone on the back steps, his cigar glowing in the twilight.

It was the same as with Aunt Minerva—my wrenching sobs, the tears and the truth.

Uncle Percy heard me to the end without a word.

"No, no," he said at last. "You're mistaken. I must have lighted the mattress myself. A spark from the pipe. Used to happen all the time in the army."

"It wasn't the mattress," I blubbered. "It was the curtains."

"Yes, perhaps. But the mattress was smouldering already. Your aunt says so."

He sighed and slowly crushed the cigar butt under his heel.

"My boy, between us men, there's no use arguing with a woman."

"I told her and she didn't believe it."

"She didn't, eh? I see."

He sighed again and then his eyes crinkled at the corners.

"Your aunt," he said, "is a great woman, a wonderful woman, but not rich in discretion. A touch of the Crawley. Ah well, no matter."

So ended my poor struggle of conscience and I had fully recovered by the time Sir Richard arrived.

The station was draped in flags and bunting, with an arch of greenery and flowers. Everyone in Emerald Vale seemed to be on the hot platform. The fire department's brass band, in scarlet uniform and fur hats, led by Chief Stott, played "The Maple Leaf Forever" as the train pulled in and the Premier of British Columbia stepped down from his private car.

I couldn't see him very well through the crowd, only the plume of white curls, the high starched collar, the cut-away coat and the flashing teeth.

Uncle Percy clasped his hand but their words were lost in the cheering.

"Speech! Speech!" the crowd bawled and Sir Richard began to talk in a quiet voice.

"My friends, in all this land of British Columbia, in all our fair Dominion, no city has a more hopeful...ah...I may say a more splendid future than Emerald Vale with its setting of natural grandeur and the...ah, ah...pioneer spirit of its people."

Again the crowd cheered and Sir Richard wiped his forehead with a silk handkerchief. I didn't understand the rest of the speech about his government but it sounded too long. At last the band played "For He's a Jolly Good Fellow" and everyone joined in the singing.

Uncle Percy led Sir Richard to a gleaming surrey from the livery stable. Old Texas Dobb was on the driver's seat in a broad-brimmed stetson and a buckskin Indian jacket, his face washed clean for once, his gray beard trimmed square across his chest. He cracked the whip. The team of matched bays started off with a jingle of harness and I followed on my cayuse.

When the surrey got to our house I sneaked through the back door and, from the kitchen, saw Sir Richard on the parlor couch. Aunt Minerva sat beside him in a new blue dress. Aunt Lizzie was pouring lemonade at the sideboard, her chains of glass beads tinkling.

Sir Richard accepted a large tumbler and sipped it with a lift of his bushy eyebrows.

"Refreshing in this hot weather," he said. "My dear lady, you're too kind."

Aunt Lizzie simpered but Sir Richard quickly placed the tumbler on the coffee table and glanced sideways at Uncle Percy.

"Yes, yes," said Uncle Percy, "the weather. Unseasonably warm. Stifling."

Marie, decked out in a black dress and white apron, had brought steaming soup to the dining room and announced that dinner was ready.

"Le diner est servi," she giggled.

"Ah, the French," Sir Richard murmured. "Charming, always charming."

I watched them work their way gradually through the soup, a pair of capons and apple pie covered with ice cream and I waited for my chance at the leavings.

"Alors, un homme gentil," Marie whispered to me as Sir Richard took Aunt Minerva's arm and escorted her back to the parlor.

37

He had seated himself on the couch beside her again and now pulled a silver case out of his pocket and lifted a cigar to his mouth.

"May I smoke?" he asked with that dazzling smile.

Aunt Minerva hesitated and looked at Uncle Percy, her plump cheeks reddening.

"Perhaps, Dick," he stammered, "we might take a little stroll in the fresh air. It's cooler outside."

"As you please, Sir Richard," said Aunt Minerva. "But it's hotter outside. And of course you may smoke. Lizzy, bring matches."

Aunt Lizzie handed Sir Richard a box of matches from the mantel. He offered a cigar to Uncle Percy and they both lighted up. The cigar smoke floated into the kitchen.

"Très gentil," Marie whispered.

Yes, I thought, one of nature's gentleman, just like Sir John and our Lord.

Without Fear or Favor

The historic provincial by-election in Emerald Vale was set for November 3, 1910. At least Mike Brindle called it historic and announced the date on his front page before the Vancouver papers got the news. Premier Sir Richard McBride had given the *Echo* a clean scoop, in return for its loyal support of the Conservative Government in Victoria.

As Brindle put it, with blackface type, "The future of British Columbia hangs on the voters of Emerald Vale. It is for them to ratify or repudiate Sir Richard's vast plan of railway construction in the rich, untapped Empire of the North. The issue is not Politics but Progress."

Under McBride's three-column picture the caption said: "Give him a New Mandate. Let Dick finish his Work."

Next to the Premier, Dandy Ryan's face appeared in a single-column cut as the Conservative Candidate. It had been taken about ten years earlier before he put on weight and lost most of his hair and didn't look much like him now. "But that wouldn't hurt him with the voters," Brindle said.

Everybody knew it was going to be a tight vote. Bob Matthews, a Liberal, had twice defeated Uncle Percy in a riding that included half a dozen small towns and villages all the way south to the American border and north to the edge of Kamloops. When Matthews was appointed to the Senate in Ottawa, leaving the seat open, Uncle Percy decided not to run again. Instead, McBride appointed him Returning Officer.

As Uncle Percy explained, he could take no part in the election campaign.

"I'm neutral, strictly neutral, a servant of the Crown under oath," he told his friends in the cosy harness room of Jake Hogarth's livery stable.

From a stall outside the open door where I was currycombing my cayuse I could easily hear the talk around the hot drum stove.

"Neutral, of course," said Brindle, "We understand."

He waved his hands like flippers and a grin split his glistening ivory face.

Dandy gave Uncle Percy a solemn wink.

"Oh, sure, neutral. All the same, your heart's in the right place, eh?"

"My principles are no secret," said Uncle Percy. "But the law will be enforced without fear or favor. Remember that!"

Hogarth was silent. When he came to town from his ranch he usually just listened, his long legs and pointed high-heel boots stretched out to the stove, his face creased like old leather. He always smelled of horses.

People said Hogarth was the richest man in the Emerald Vale riding, with many business interests outside it, and he had managed all the Conservative Party's campaigns.

Now he gulped down his whisky and poured himself another glass, neat.

"Get this," he drawled. "We're up against the toughest fight ever. The Grits have us beat to a fare-thee-well."

"No, no," said Doc Foster, the vet, his white billy goat's beard wagging vigorously. "She's tough but we can fix it."

"Fix it?" cried Dandy. "Christ, them Grits fix everything. Crooks, the whole damn kit and caboodle. Look at Laurier, look at

Sifton, look at that little squirt Mackenzie what's his name..."

"Name's King," Brindle grunted.

"King or queen, he's a squirt."

"I can't offer any advice," said Uncle Percy, "but haven't you forgotten the real danger?"

"Like what?" Hogarth demanded.

"Like Copper Ridge. It went solid Grit last time and the town has grown by half with all those Italian miners. Over three hundred voters on the new list, enough to swing it even if you carry the Vale hands down. But that's your business, not mine."

Dandy's face puckered in deep thought.

"The Ridge, yeah. Solid Grit ever since Laurier built that fancy post office."

"McBride give 'em a bigger court house," said Foster. "One of Dick's speeches and we'll swing the Ridge."

"Speeches won't help none," said Dandy. "Them dagoes only speak Eye-talian and the Grits can buy 'em, five dollars a vote, easy."

"And print fake ballots and stuff the boxes," Brindle muttered.

"So they did last time and beat me, though I couldn't prove it." said Uncle Percy. "But this time I've appointed honest deputies up there and the Provincials will be watching on election day."

Old Texas Dobb, the stable boss, had been listening from his bunk in the corner, half asleep behind a tangle of white whiskers. At the mention of the Provincial Police he raised himself on his elbow.

"Balls! Why that bunch couldn't track an elephant bleeding to death in ten feet of snow."

Dobb had been a tracker, train robber and sheriff in Texas, or so he claimed, and his opinions carried weight.

"The ballots are safe at the Ridge," said Uncle Percy. "The risk lies elsewhere."

Brindle scratched his three chins.

"Elsewhere! Where's elsewhere?"

"It's not my affair but the train leaves the Ridge for the Vale an hour after the polls close. The boxes will be on it. And it stops half an hour at Willow Creek for water. Does that suggest some..ah...possibilities?"

"You're damn right it does!" Hogarth growled "The crew's eatin' supper at the Creek. The baggage car's open. Plenty of time to stuff the boxes. That's where they done it last time I bet."

Dandy banged his glass on the table.

"I get it! Our boys'll be at the Creek first and watch the boxes."

He winked at the others.

"And maybe do a little fixin' of their own, eh, to make it fair and square all round?"

Uncle Percy gave him a hard look."No, you don't get it. And if there's any tampering with the ballots I'll have you all in jail. Read the law. Good night, gentlemen."

He drained his whisky and put on his overcoat and walked out the side door.

"Now what's that all about?" Brindle demanded.

"Hell, Percy don't mean it," said Dandy.

Hogarth began to pace up and down the room.

"Oh, he means it all right. He's tellin' us something."

"But what?" Foster grumbled. "Makes no sense for the Grits to monkey with the Ridge votes. They're safe as houses up there."

"Not any more they aren't," said Brindle. "Against Dandy alone they might be. Not against McBride."

Hogarth paused to spit his tobacco juice at the stove with a hissing sound.

"Read the law, Percy says. The law, eh? Listen, Dandy, leave it to me. You can't take any chances."

"Well now, I don't know..."

"Keep out of it, that's all."

Hogarth beckoned to Brindle.

"Come on, I wanna talk this thing over."

They both left by the side door and headed for the Majestic bar.

A week later the Liberals held their convention in the hall above

44

Grimshaw's Central Emporium. Delegates came from every district of the Emerald Vale riding, a dozen from Copper Ridge, led by the famous Roary Wallace—a giant, he looked to me, with a flaming red beard, steel-blue eyes and a queer, fuzzy Scotch accent. In his Caledonian hotel at the Ridge, I'd been told, he could take on three or four men and throw them out of the bar. After seeing him I didn't doubt it. And after hearing him I knew why he was called Roary. He didn't talk. He roared.

Wendell Simpson was the only man nominated and he spoke for an hour on the corruption of the McBride Government, railway graft and the evils of the drink trade. When the convention gave him a unanimous vote nobody was surprised. He had been working for it ever since Bob Matthews went to the Senate.

I often bought candy in Simpson's drug store and liked him because I always got some extra pieces, free. He was a friend to all the kids in town and a fancy dresser, wearing stiff white collars like Macdonald, Laurier and McBride, and the same curls around his neck, too. But they were black and his face was chubby, pink and unlined like a baby's.

At Ma Hislop's boarding house the other bachelors called him Wendy and teased him about his strict temperance views and his solos in the Methodist Church on Sundays. He took this joshing with his baby smile and never stopped talking about temperance and prohibition to all his customers and anyone else willing to listen. Among the Conservatives he was known as Windy and Brindle said he was a pansy. I didn't know what that meant.

After the Liberal convention broke up most of the delegates had dinner with Simpson in the Kozy Kettle Kafe. But I saw Roary and some of the men from the Ridge sneaking in the back door of the Plaza Hotel and I heard that roaring voice in the alley.

"Yon Wendy's a braw lad but a leetle bit daft aboot gude whusky. Ah weel, nae doot he'll do fine, y'ken, fer politics."

Next day Dandy and his friends met in the harness room but Uncle Percy wasn't there. He said it wouldn't look right for the returning officer to be seen much with politicians.

45

"I can't make it out," Dandy complained. "Roary Wallace backin' Windy Simpson on temperance and prohibition! Why, for God's sake?"

"Because," said Foster, "Windy's got pull with Laurier and Laurier's got the patronage."

"But prohibition splits the Grits."

"Parties always split," Brindle grunted. "Politics is a funny game. You can't choose your friends."

"And Roary's got the votes." Hogarth told them. "The dagoes don't like him but he scares 'em and half the Ridge owes him money."

"Lucky we only got Windy to beat," said Dandy.

"That's where you're dead wrong. Windy's no push-over. He'll get the whole temperance crowd in the Vale."

Dandy snorted.

"Temperance crowd? Hell, that's jest the wimmin."

"If wimmin had the vote you wouldn't have a Chinaman's chance," Tex croaked from his bunk.

"Well, they haven't" Foster chortled, "and their men folk likes a drink, same as anybody. Most of 'em won't vote for Windy."

"A lot will," said Brindle. "Why not? They know Windy's prohibition talk won't change anything. And he'll have the patronage from Laurier."

Hogarth spat his tobacco juice and it sizzled against the stove.

"The Ridge, yeah. And Willow Creek. They'll stuff the ballots if we let 'em. But I'll tend to it."

He glared at Dandy.

"Don't go round knockin' Windy. It won't pay."

"No personalities," said Brindle. "Stick to the issues. The railway policy, northern development, let Dick finish his work. A clean campaign. There's the ticket."

Dandy's jowls quivered.

"Clean? When the Grits always play it dirty? And Windy, that creepin' Jeezler! Sings in church, dyes his hair and curls it with tongs like Laurier."

46

"Like Miss Stella," said Tex.

Dandy shot him an ugly look.

"Leave her out of it y'hear?"

There was a sudden pause in the talk with everybody staring at the stove. Then Hogarth got to his feet and put on his sheepskin coat.

"Sure, sure, Dandy," he said. "She's out of it. And you, too. Let me handle this thing my own way, see? Legal, strictly legal."

When I went home for supper Aunt Minerva seemed to have a touch of the Crawley and worked it off on Uncle Percy.

"Your precious Dandy! Why, the man's an ignoramus, a low vulgarian."

"A publican," Aunt Minerva whinnied. "And you know what our Lord said about publicans."

"Different times, different customs," Uncle Percy murmured. "At least he's no hypocrite like Windy Simpson."

Aunt Minerva sniffed.

"That awful creature! And he sings solos for the Methodists— falsetto. Oh, how I hate and loathe and despise politics!"

"But they're unavoidable, my dear, even in the Old Country."

I learned quite a bit about politics in the next few weeks and they improved Dandy no end. On Brindle's advice he went to Vancouver and came back with a new rig-out. Instead of his checked suits and flowered vests he was wearing dark blue serge and a black bowler. His hair was plastered across the bald spot, his jowls powdered, his nails manicured, and he smelled strong of perfume.

His friends looked him over in the harness room and said he'd do.

"But remember," Brindle warned him, "you're the people's candidate. Jest the ordinary citizen, the common man. None of Windy's highfalutin' talk. Stick to McBride and the railways."

"Yeah, and remember," said Hogarth, "you can't buy drinks for anybody till the election's over. I looked it up and it's agin the law."

After that Dandy stayed out of his Majestic Bar but I noticed a

47

lot of men drinking there every night with Brindle and Hogarth.

The *Echo* was full of political news and Brindle's long editorials. He couldn't find space to report the Liberal manifesto and he didn't catch a paragraph at the bottom of a column on the back page. It recalled that "Gladstone was the Father of Liberalism and the greatest statesman in British history."

Paul Jessup was fired and came back to work as usual next morning.

Windy got his manifesto printed in Kamloops and paid kids to drop a copy at every door in the Vale riding. It promised Real Democracy, the Return of Government to the People, Progress and Prosperity. In red type the voters were urged to "Smash the McBride Machine and End all Patronage." The Drink Trade wasn't mentioned.

"He's goin' easy on booze till the polls close," said Hogarth, "Roary warned him off."

"It sounds good all the same," Dandy allowed. "Windy's got the gift of the gab."

"Not him," said Brindle. "Laurier wrote it. That's his style—oily, flashy, French. But the Grits are smart."

Hogarth, I thought, was smart, too. He let the Grits hire his best team of matched bays and the new surrey from the livery stable and Simpson used them to drive around the riding with bundles of his manifesto.

"Folks like a good sport," Hogarth explained. "And Dandy comes from the States. The American angle don't help any."

Dandy jumped up and spilled his drink.

"Naturalized, ain't I? Got my papers twelve years back. Jest as good a Canadian as anybody and done more for this town."

He sat down again.

"Oh well, give Windy the godamn team. But he's no sport. A pansy, I tellya."

Dandy travelled everywhere across the riding in his crimson Reo. It thumped and shook and lurched through the mud but made fast time, almost twenty miles an hour. Hogarth did the driving so the candidate could leap down to the sidewalks of the villages and shake hands with the voters or the ranchers on the side roads. Sometimes I rode in the back seat and handed out the Conservative pamphlets to anyone who'd take them.

One day we started at dawn and drove fifty miles to Copper Ridge where I'd never been before. It was a queer town with high wooden towers above the mine shafts, rows of shanties on the hill and a single narrow street beside a stream of filthy water.

"Talk to 'em about the railway and McBride and jobs up north," Hogarth told Dandy. "No use talkin' politics to this bunch."

Dandy bustled along the street, stopping the miners and shaking their hands but most of them didn't look interested and few seemed to understand English.

"Eye-talians, dagoes," Dandy grumbled when he got back in the car.

"It's Roary's town all right," said Hogarth.

As we drove past the Caledonian Hotel a red beard was pressed against the window of the bar room. I thought Roary was laughing at us.

On the way home we ate some sandwiches in the dingy lunch room across the street from the Willow Creek station. Then Dandy and Hogarth talked to the railway agent over his counter—a shriveled little man with a mean rat's face and clicking teeth, the work of a clumsy dentist. He gave them a timetable but said the train from the Ridge was often late these days when it stopped at the Creek for water.

Foster met us at the stable that night with bad news.

"They're up to their old tricks. Got the bohunks cullin' Windy."

I'd heard of that trick. In the woods where the Swedes and Finns hacked ties for the railways the boss culled the bad ones by marking a cross on them with a blue pencil. When Uncle Percy had run in the last election the tiehacks were persuaded to put a cross on the ballot beside the Liberal candidate's name to show they were against him. Hogarth figured that Uncle Percy had been culled out of nearly a hundred votes.

"And they'll do it again," Dandy growled.

"No they won't," said Hogarth. "I'll fix 'em."

All this time Uncle Percy kept away from the harness room and rented an empty store for an office to organize the election without fear or favor. He even paid Joe Scully, a strong Liberal, to print the ballots on his job press. Brindle wanted the business for the *Echo* but admitted that the returning officer must be neutral.

"It's the look of the thing," he said.

"I don't get it," Dandy complained. "Monkey business at the Ridge. Fake ballots, likely. Bohunks cullin' Windy. The whole works and you let 'em get away with it."

"Leave it to me," Hogarth told him. "Best you don't know too much."

Next day Brindle came puffing and gloating to the harness room with a telegram from Victoria. McBride had promised to make a speech in Emerald Vale.

"That settles it!" said Dandy. "Dick never loses elections."

Hogarth looked doubtful as he cut a chew from his tobacco plug.

"Don't be too sure. Remember the Ridge."

"But we'll make Dick's meeting the biggest thing that ever happened in the Vale," said Brindle.

The Conservatives hired the hall above the Central Emporium and dressed it up in red, white and blue bunting, with a Union Jack on the wall behind the platform. Brindle wrote a short, snappy speech for Dandy and made him memorize it, word for word, with special emphasis on the American angle. It sounded fine to me when he recited it in the harness room.

The hall was packed for the great night and a lot of people waited at the door of the Emporium just to catch a glimpse of McBride. From a back seat, between Foster and Tex, I could hear the cheering outside and we all stood up and cheered, too, when the Premier came down the aisle. Everybody recognized the high stiff collar, the white curls and the flashing smile.

On the platform he put his arm around Dandy Ryan's shoulder and that set off more cheers. Then Brindle, as chairman, introduced the candidate.

"Before we hear from our distinguished guest and beloved Prime Minister." he said, "I present your fellow citizen of Emerald Vale, this city's best booster, who carries the standard of the grand old Conservative Party to certain victory!"

"Hear! Hear!" McBride shouted and clapped his hands and we all clapped with him.

Dandy got to his feet in his new Vancouver suit. His face was as crimson as the Reo but his words came out pretty close to the way Brindle had written them.

"You folks all know I'm here because I chose Canada fer my country of my own free will, irregardless. I stand before you as a proud subject of His Majesty the King, I stand fer Emerald Vale, fer Dick McBride, fer British Columbia, fer the Dominion and fer the Empire!"

McBride and everybody clapped again.

And then, as I'd seen him do it at rehearsals in the harness room, Dandy turned and pointed at the Union Jack.

"I care not who the man may be, whether he come from England or Scotland or Ireland or Italy or the United States of America where I come from, if he should trample and spit on that sacred flag, I say damn him!"

More cheers shook the hall.

"Go it, Dandy!" Foster yelled.

"Balls!" said Tex but in all that noise I was the only one who heard him.

McBride covered his face with a handkerchief and blew his nose. He was overcome with emotion, I guessed. But he soon recovered and grasped Dandy's hand and began his own speech.

"It's an honor, a privilege, indeed a heart-warming pleasure for me to be here with my good old friend and loyal Conservative, Andy Bryan..."

There was a titter in the crowd but McBride didn't seem to notice his slip and went straight on.

"Friends, all friends, tonight I must speak frankly, even bluntly, because the people of Emerald Vale will decide a question too serious, much too serious, for politics. Is the railway to be built to the treasury of the North or abandoned in craven fear of British Columbia's future—yes, I may say, its splendid destiny? In this election, the most important in my rather long experience, the whole Dominion awaits your verdict!"

He hunched his shoulders, leaned forward and dropped his voice almost to a whisper.

"And so I ask you to lay aside all political sentiment and vote for the interests of our Province and your own. And I remind you that the Liberal Party has never supported railways and even tried to stop the C.P.R. that carried our nation from sea to sea."

The crowd yelled louder than ever.

I can't remember the rest of McBride's speech, only the last words.

"My government, my plans, my mandate—yes, and all the hopes of our fair province are now committed to the people of this historic riding of Emerald Vale and I know they will not betray that trust."

At that the crowd exploded. Someone began to play the piano and we sang "God Save the King" and McBride, still smiling and shaking hands, escaped to sleep in his private railway car.

On election day I was allowed to miss school and run messages for Uncle Percy between his office and the four polling stations. In the afternoon I passed the livery stable as the Reo, its engine already thumping and smoking, started out for Willow Creek. Hogarth was at the wheel, Brindle beside him, Foster and Tex in the back seat under a buffalo robe.

From the sidewalk Dandy was shouting into Hogarth's ear.

"Grab them ballot boxes before the sonsabitches get their hands on em! Don't break no laws if you don't have to..."

"Leave it to us," said Hogarth. "And fer Christ sake shut up!"

He yanked the gear lever and the Reo went shuddering and clanking down the street.

The polls closed at seven o'clock and the sealed ballot boxes of

52

Emerald Vale were fetched to Uncle Percy's office and piled behind his desk. But he wouldn't start counting the votes till the boxes from the Ridge and some outlying polls were collected. Dandy and Windy and their friends stood around the office, the Tories on one side, the Grits on the other. Nobody said much.

It was after eleven when I heard the clank of the Reo in the lane. Dandy heard it, too, and slipped out the back door and I followed him. Hogarth was alone in the driver's seat. He looked shook up and one of his eyes was closed and swollen.

"What happened?" Dandy gasped.

"We had a little scrap with Roary and his boys, that's all."

"Where's the boxes?"

"On the train. They'll be here pretty soon."

"You left 'em to the Grits?"

"They're safe. Brindle's with 'em and Doc Foster and Tex and the policeman."

"Was they opened?"

"Sure they was. Roary pawed over the ballots pretty good before we bust into the baggage car."

"You let him get ahead of you?"

"Sure we did."

Dandy's jowls swelled out like wattles on a turkey.

"You what?"

"We let 'em. Then we stuck the ballots in the boxes and nailed 'em down."

"Even the fake ones?"

"The whole works. Don't worry. Everything's under control."

"Under control? Why, Jesus, you..."

Before he could say any more the train whistled across the bridge. Dandy jumped in beside Hogarth and they went clattering away to the station.

The rest of us waited in the office till the Reo came up the street again with Brindle, Foster and Tex in the back seat. Each of them held a big green wooden box on his knees. Behind them, in a rig from the livery stable, I saw Roary and some strangers.

Uncle Percy pushed through the crowd in front of his office.

Roary leaped to the sidewalk.

"A bludy outrage!" he roared. "They stole the ballots! By Cot almighty we'll have the law on 'em..."

"Calm yourself, Mr. Wallace," said Uncle Percy.

Roary thrust out his flaming beard.

"We was only lookin' over the votes to see they was counted proper and then..."

Brindle eased himself down from the Reo. He'd lost his hat and there was a purple lump on the side of his bald head.

"It's a lie!" he gasped. "They'd broken the boxes open."

"That's right!" cried Foster. "Ballots all over the floor."

Two strangers alighted from the rig. I recognized the station agent at Willow Creek, the shriveled face and the clicking store teeth. The second man wore the khaki uniform of the Provincial Police. He was huge like Roary. Under his clipped mustache I noticed a trickle of blood on his chin.

"We'll settle this inside," said Uncle Percy.

Everybody trooped after him, shoving and yammering, until he sat quietly at his desk the three wooden boxes beside him.

"Now the facts, gentlemen," he said. "Just the facts."

The policeman elbowed his way to the desk. His jaw was set hard, his voice brisk.

"Constable Denis Horrigan, sir, Willow Creek. On information received I entered the baggage car at nine p.m. approximately. A fight was in progress. I stopped it."

"And the ballots?" Uncle Percy asked.

The station agent clenched his teeth and spoke up in a quavering tone.

"The crew and me, five of us, was eatin' supper in the lunch room and nobody seen them fellas. They must of come in the train from the Ridge and got at the boxes and then the others came in the automobile and started fightin' fer the boxes..."

"Na, na" cried Roary. "We was only..."

"Count the ballots!" Hogarth yelled from the back of the crowd.

54

"There's over a hundred too many from the Ridge."

"Indeed?" said Uncle Percy. "I'll see to that in due course. And you, Mr. Simpson?"

Windy had been pushed to the wall and the pink was all drained out of his cheeks.

"I know nothing about it," he sputtered. "On my word."

"No one questions your word, sir. But Mr. Wallace broke the seals, opened the boxes, took possession of the ballots. He says so himself. Accordingly, I must reject all the Copper Ridge votes. The law gives me no alternative."

"We'll take it to the courts!" Roary bellowed. "Aye, to the Preevy Council in Loondon..."

"That's your privilege, Mr. Wallace. And you may petition the courts to order a new election if you choose."

"Och mon, we'll do it, never fear!"

"And I shall report to the Attorney General in Victoria. He can decide whether to prosecute you for a very serious offense under the Elections Act of British Columbia."

Uncle Percy stood up and put on his overcoat.

"Tomorrow the votes will be counted. Except those from the Ridge, of course."

Next morning he counted them on a long table. Dandy and Windy watched him with their friends but Roary had gone home to the Ridge. By noon the final count for the whole Emerald Vale riding gave Dandy 1,365 votes and Windy 1,307.

The ballots were put back into the last box and Uncle Percy locked it.

"As returning officer," he said, "I declare Mr. Ryan elected"

Afterwards, in the harness room, Dandy uncorked a big bottle that popped and spilled on the floor.

"Too bad Percy isn't here," said Brindle. "But it wouldn't look right."

Dandy grinned over his foaming glass at Hogarth.

"Now I get it. You and Percy cooked it up from the start. Waited till the sonsabitches busted the boxes, called that police fella, trapped 'em, by God!"

Hogarth's tobacco juice hissed against the stove.

"No, they trapped themselves, like we figgered. The policeman happened to be around there on information received. You heard him say so. Lucky."

"All Percy told us was remember the law," Brindle snickered. "We read it but the Grits forgot. Yeah, lucky."

Dandy had a sudden idea that seemed to worry him.

"What if they go to court for a new election?"

"And get jailed fer hanky-panky with the votes?" Hogarth said, "Not a chance."

Dandy poured himself another drink and grinned at his friends.

"Well, Percy was right. Without fear or favor. The old bastard."

But it turned out that he was wrong. A week later they somehow got hold of the boxes from the Ridge and counted the ballots in the harness room with the doors closed. Dandy had a lead of 13 over Windy.

"Huh." Foster grumbled. "The Ridge wouldn't of changed nothin' after all. We was only wastin' our time."

"Politics," said Brindle, "is a funny game."

The Epic of Petit Trudeau

Sir Wilfrid Laurier put Emerald Vale on the map of Canada just before he lost the election of 1911. Even the Conservatives agreed about that. But he hadn't planned it and couldn't have done it without Petit Trudeau who ran faster and drank more beer than any other Canadian. Or so we all believed.

Uncle Percy first suggested that the Liberal Prime Minister should be invited to the celebration of the Queen's Birthday on May 24 and the foot race for the championship of Canada if not the world.

The men in the harness room didn't think much of the idea.

"It's both ridiculous and absurd," said Mike Brindle.

"And him a damn Grit," Dandy Ryan added. "French, too. Always was, always will be. That's Laurier."

Uncle Percy polished his glasses with a handkerchief and looked thoughtful.

"True," he admitted. "But Laurier happens to be Prime Minister and he can't help being French. And we can't change him till the election."

"That won't be long," Tex croaked from his bunk. "Else he wouldn't be comin' out west to size up the vote."

"With aces up his sleeve," Doc Foster grumbled. "Free trade and all that Yankee talk. Wreckin' the country."

"True," Uncle Percy repeated. "But the Queen's Birthday has nothing to do with the election. Victoria never played politics—a woman of good sense. She hated Gladstone. Then again, Laurier and Petit are both French. So Laurier watches his compatriot win the race. A nice sentimental touch. A kind of epic, in fact."

"Epic?" Foster demanded. "What's a epic? And suppose he don't win?"

"No chance of that," said Uncle Percy, "so long as he's in shape. Didn't he win in Nelson and Cranbrook last fall with no training?"

"Petit's not in shape," Brindle grunted. "Hasn't run a yard this spring."

Petit seemed in good shape to me. He was shoeing a Clydesdale in the blacksmith shop behind the livery stable and looked almost as big as the horse. That's why everyone called him Petit. In French, I'd found out at school, Petit means small and I took the name for a joke.

Nobody knew Petit's real name anyhow and he didn't care. Since coming from Rimouski with his sister, Marie, our cook, he'd scarcely learned a word of English and seldom said anything, even in French. But he could run a mile in five minutes by Uncle Percy's stop watch and the *Echo* christened him The Emerald Vale Flier.

You wouldn't guess his speed, though, by looking at him. He was almost as fat as Dandy, six feet four high and under a tangle of black curls his round, shiny face was always fixed in a shy little grin.

With his nearly three hundred pounds he held a lot of beer and stayed cold sober. At the Vale's autumn fair the visitors from out of town had watched him drink at least a gallon at the Majestic bar just before the race and bet heavily against him. But Petit left the best runners from Kamloops, Kelowna and Merritt a hundred yards behind. His local backers won a pile that day.

Now the men in the harness room watched his hammer rise and

60

fall, the muscles swelling in his bare arms.

"Petit's not in shape," Brindle said again. "And they've got that new fella in Kamloops, name of Jed Mossop. He's mighty good."

I'd heard of Jed. They claimed he'd even broken Petit's record and the papers were calling him the Kamloops Komet. But Uncle Percy didn't believe that story.

"His time wasn't clocked," he explained. "Not officially. All the same, Petit needs training. No more beer."

"Wait a minute," said Dandy. "You cut him down too sudden and you throw him off his stride."

"No more beer," Uncle Percy insisted. "I ought to know a little about training. Rowed for Oxford in the seventies and we beat Cambridge a full length. No beer. That's the Oxford method."

"Petit'll do," said Foster. "My money's on him."

"And mine," Uncle Percy agreed. "He comes of old stock, Norman peasants, mostly illiterate but strong. Quebec's full of Trudeaus and I dare say some may be brighter than poor Petit."

Jake Hogarth had listened without saying a word, chewing his tobacco and spitting at the stove. Now he began to pace up and down the room.

"The way I see it," he said at last, "politics don't signify. Laurier comes to Kamloops next month and if we get him here it'll be the makin' of the town. Crowds from all over. Special train from Vancouver. Reporters from the eastern papers. The whole country talkin' about the Vale. Great fer business. Great fer the Majestic."

"Yeah, there's that," Dandy conceded. "So long as I don't have to meet him."

"But you have to meet him," said Uncle Percy. "A member of the Legislature can't insult the Prime Minister even if he's in the wrong party."

"And Windy Simpson has to be there," Hogarth went on. "Laurier'll expect to see the Grit boss."

"Over my dead body," Dandy protested.

"You got to be reasonable," said Hogarth. "It's fer the town, remember. You'll meet the train. You'll take Laurier and Windy and the rest of 'em in the Reo. Pictures in all the papers. Make your reputation clear across the country."

"Oh well," Dandy mumbled. "But only fer the town."

As Chairman of the Celebration Committee, Uncle Percy telegraphed an invitation to Laurier and the training of Petit began that evening.

The Emerald Vale Flier gulped eight pints at the Majestic, against Uncle Percy's warning. Then, taking off his boots and socks and all his clothes except his pants, he prepared to run three times, a measured mile, around the rodeo field outside town. At the starting point he warmed up by dancing on the grass and the beer seemed to pour out of him in rivers of sweat. With a hoarse bellow he lowered his head and charged like a bull.

"See?" cried Dandy as Petit came pounding smoothly past the finishing line. "He's in good shape. Runs on beer. The hell with the Oxford method."

Uncle Percy had kept his eyes on his stop watch.

"It won't do," he said. "Five minutes, seventeen seconds. No more beer."

Only a born diplomat like Uncle Percy could have cut Petit off his beer. But after some argument the Flier moved to Hogarth's ranch at The Bend with a hundred dollars to make up for his lost wages in the blacksmith shop and the promise of five hundred if he beat the Komet. Tex was sent along to see that he stayed on the wagon.

By this time Laurier had accepted the invitation of the Celebration Committee by telegram. He told the reporters in Ottawa that he looked forward with pleasure to the athletic contest at the Vale and the traditional hospitality of the West.

"What he's lookin' fer," said Foster, "is votes. Draggin' the Queen's birthday into politics already."

Everything seemed to be going fine but I could see that Uncle Percy was worried. He warned Brindle that the public build-up of Petit had been overdone when the odds on him stood at three to one, even in Kamloops. There wasn't much chance of big winnings

62

for his backers.

In the next issue of the *Echo* Brindle printed a brief item reporting that Petit had strained his left ankle. This drove the odds down a bit and they fell again when the *Kamloops Sentinel* announced that Jed Mossop was training eight hours a day and had been clocked at a second under five minutes.

"Jest lies," said Tex. "Only a horse could do it. A thoroughbred."

Some strangers, decked out in fancy clothes and a lot of jewelry, drifted through the Vale and bought drinks for everybody in the Majestic. They tried to see Petit training but Tex wouldn't let them past the gate at the ranch and he turned away three reporters from Vancouver.

All this secrecy encouraged more betting on the Flier. The odds reached five to one. Next week a short paragraph on the back page of the *Echo* said Petit had "suffered a minor heart ailment which his medical advisors do not regard as serious."

That same night Petit escaped from the ranch and ran seven miles to town, barefoot. At the Plaza Hotel, the Grit hang-out, he guzzled a dozen pints before Dandy arrived and found him sitting on the steps, wearing only his pants and singing "Alouette" in a sad French voice. Dandy wrapped a blanket around him and took him to the ranch in the Reo.

News of the seven-mile run got into all the papers. The *Vancouver Gazette*'s sport page called Petit "The Beer Barrel on Legs" and the *Calgary Herald* wrote a piece about "The Fountain of Furious Froth." His odds kept edging up.

Uncle Percy had turned sulky and irritable, even with Aunt Minerva. After watching Petit's daily work-out, he told the Celebration Committee that there must be a traitor in the camp.

"Petit's still getting beer," he complained. "You can see it coming out of every pore. He's slowing down."

"I'll take care of that," said Hogarth.

He moved out to his ranch with Tex and together they guarded Petit day and night. But Uncle Percy was still worried. His bets were high, I guessed.

A week before the race he went to Kamloops on business and watched Jed training. When he came home his mood had changed. He was cheerful again. The Komet, he reported, was over-trained and fading, and I heard him promise Aunt Minerva to take her for a trip to Vancouver on his winnings. She was delighted but wondered if these bets were quite fitting. He assured her that the race was good, clean amateur sport.

Windy Simpson wasn't a betting man but his Grits had been busy preparing for Laurier's arrival. They stretched a banner across the main street to declare that "Emerald Vale Salutes Canada's Great Liberal Chieftain."

Brindle said this was cheap, piddling politics but he wrote in a generous editorial that "While we judge him to be the architect of the nation's future ruin, the Prime Minister, who will soon be removed from office, is welcome in our city for a non-partisan Royal Anniversary."

On the afternoon of May 24 the special train pulled in with five extra coaches from Kamloops, two Pullmans from Vancouver and Laurier's private car at the end.

Dandy had left his Reo back of the station, the engine running. He stood with Uncle Percy and Windy at the front edge of the platform, all of them stiff and nervous. Hogarth, Brindle and Foster were in the surrey, Tex holding the reins. I eased my pony close to them to get a clear view of the train. Not so many people had turned out as for Sir Richard McBride but it was a big crowd in a Conservative town.

The Kamloops passengers got off first and among them I recognized Jed Mossop from his pictures in the papers—a short man, hardly more than a boy, with a pinched, hollow face and a squirrel's buck teeth. The crowd recognized him, too, but only a few of them cheered the Komet.

Then a tall man in a gray frock coat stepped from the last car and a shout went up for Laurier. He seemed much older than his portrait in Windy's drug store and paler, almost as white as his high, starched collar. When he lifted his top hat I saw that his gray curls were just like McBride's around a glistening bald head.

Some reporters followed, scribbling in notebooks. Half a dozen photographers lugged their cameras and tripods along the platform. Then I noticed a plump young fellow with chubby pink cheeks and a wide grin. He was dressed the same as Laurier and bobbed after him like a puppy.

"By God," Hogarth shouted above the noise of the crowd, "I believe it's that squirt Mackenzie."

"Name's King," said Brindle. "He's Minister of Labour."

"That's a laugh", Tex growled. "Never done a day's work in his life. Look at his hands."

King's tiny hands were fluttering out to touch any others he saw in front of them and he grinned at everybody.

Uncle Percy, Dandy and Windy had taken off their hats and stood stiffly in line as Laurier approached. He shook their hands but in all the cheering I couldn't hear what he said. The three official hosts led him to the Reo. Dandy, purple and sweating, took the wheel with Laurier beside him, Uncle Percy and Windy in the back seat. The Reo snorted away to the rodeo field.

By the time I got there a tight circle of wagons and buggies was drawn around the race track. Cowboys had come in from all the ranches and Indians and their squaws and kids from the Reserve.

Laurier was sitting on a long bench, Aunt Minerva to his right, under a green parasol, Uncle Percy to his left. Marie, Petit's sister, was beside Mackenzie King in a scarlet dress and a floppy hat of feathers. Dandy and Windy were together and they both looked grim.

Hogarth, Brindle, Foster and Tex had squeezed through the crowd to the back of the bench and I kept with them.

At the far side of the track the two runners had changed their clothes in separate tents. Jed, in blue shorts and spiked shoes, walked over to the bench, the muscles of his knotted little body rippling, his buck teeth bared in a smile or a snarl. Laurier rose to take his hand.

"Good luck," he said, "to Kamloops."

"Playin' to the Kamloops vote," Foster muttered but his words were drowned in a sudden roar from the crowd as Petit shambled to the bench. He was barefoot and naked except for a scrap of yellow pants around his middle. They were too tight for him, though he seemed to have lost half his old weight. The baby smile was gone and he had a dazed look.

"Sir Wilfrid," said Uncle Percy, "allow me to present your famous compatriot from Quebec, Petit Trudeau, better known as the Flier."

"All Canadians are my compatriots," Laurier replied, a little sharply, I thought, but he took Petit's huge hand in both his own and added: *Mon brave, bon chance!*"

"That's French," Foster explained. "Playin' to the Vale vote, too."

Petit just gaped down at his bare feet and wriggled his toes in the dust.

"He ain't right," Dandy whispered to Uncle Percy. "I told you— dried him out too quick. Your bloody Oxford method."

"Nonsense," Uncle Percy whispered back. "He's in the pink. Nerves, that's all."

The two runners walked across the field to the starting point. Laurier leaned forward, his gray gloves cupped on the silver knob of his cane. King was trying to talk in French to Marie but she didn't seem to understand him and only blushed and giggled.

No sound came from the crowd as Petit and Jed knelt side by side. Then I saw a spurt of flame and heard a pistol crack.

Jed leaped ahead, his short legs flashing like a pair of scissors. Petit rose slowly to his feet and stood still, his mouth open, his eyes fixed on the ground.

"What's got into him?" Hogarth grumbled.

"Not beer anyways." said Tex.

"Just wait," Uncle Percy muttered but the watch was shaking in his hand.

Sure enough, at that moment Petit lowered his head and charged. I knew he was all right now. His long legs moved like the driving shafts of a locomotive and on the curve he passed Jed. By the end of the first lap he'd gained a lead of about twenty yards.

Laurier and the others were on their feet. Dandy made hoarse choking sounds. Aunt Minerva waved her parasol and howled, "Go it, Petit, go it!" Marie was screaming in French.

Uncle Percy slumped alone on the bench, his face twitching. No one else noticed him and I didn't know what was wrong. Maybe, I thought, he's sick with a heart attack or something but I couldn't keep my eyes off the race.

The Komet gained a few yards on the second lap but Petit was still far ahead at the start of the third. Everybody was yelling, even Windy. Laurier didn't feel it when Aunt Minerva slapped his shoulder and threw her parasol into the air. Dandy shouted in Uncle Percy's ear, "You done it, old pal, you done it! The Oxford method!"

Uncle Percy hadn't moved. He stared at his watch and let it drop to dangle with his glasses between his legs.

The thing happened near the end of the last lap. I saw Petit wobble sideways. His legs crumpled under him and he sank to the ground. A groan went up from the crowd, then silence, broken by a shriek from Marie.

"*Courage, ma chère*," said Laurier as she collapsed in his arms.

Petit's body unfolded slowly till he lay flat, gazing up at the sky. The Komet passed him without a glance and sprinted across the finishing line. A thin cheer came from the Kamloops visitors.

King was peering blankly at Petit.

"Why would Trudeau do that?" he asked. "Is the poor fellow dead?"

Petit wasn't dead. Hogarth and Brindle had run out on the track with the reporters and camera men. They lifted Petit to his feet and he stumbled to his tent. Jed was carried off the field on the shoulders of his friends.

At this terrible moment Uncle Percy's courage made me proud of him. He put his glasses back on his nose and the stop watch in his pocket. The wild look was gone as he turned to Laurier.

"Mr. Prime Minister, I'm sorry your boy from Quebec didn't win. The luck of the game."

"*Mais non*," said Laurier. "All Canadians are the same to me." Seeing the tears on Marie's cheeks, he dabbed them gently with a silk handkerchief.

"Most extraordinary," King murmured. "Unfortunate." Dandy said nothing. But now he snatched the top hat from Uncle Percy's head and stamped it flat under his shoe.

"Oxford!" he bawled and pushed his way through the crowd to his Reo.

When the Celebration Committee met in the harness room a few days later they were quiet and gloomy. No wonder, I thought. They had all lost a pile of money on the race. Only Uncle Percy was missing from the circle.

"I can't figger what happened to Petit," Hogarth said at last. "It don't make sense."

Dandy glared at the others.

"You know what I think? I think Percy seen he'd dried Petit out like I always told him. So he sneaks over to Kamloops and switches his bets and puts 'em on that godamn Komet fella, and big odds, too. Oh yeah, Percy looks mighty flush these days."

Brindle jumped up and pounded his glass on the table.

"No, no! Percy wouldn't do it, not Percy. Ridiculous and absurd."

Of course it was ridiculous and absurd. But Uncle Percy had kept his promise and taken Aunt Minerva on a trip to Vancouver. She was wearing a new velvet dress when they came home and he brought me a bridle for my pony of real tooled leather and a snaffle bit.

At the autumn fair in Kelowna Petit drank a gallon of beer and ran a mile in less than five minutes, the Komet fifty yards behind him. That was a world record all right and an epic. But the time hadn't been officially clocked.

The Canadian Saga

Uncle Percy hadn't expected to play Louis Riel in the movies or ride Jake Hogarth's bay stallion in the battle scene. The whole thing was a kind of accident.

I missed the arrival of Hamilton Garrett because I was in Kamloops getting new bands on my crooked front teeth. But when I came home next morning they told me at the livery stable that Garrett was the biggest man in Hollywood, some town in California. And when I sneaked into the back room of Uncle Percy's office I found him talking to the famous director. They were too keyed up to notice me behind the door.

Garrett was a big man, all right, well over six feet and seemed to be bursting out of his fancy checked suit. His head was bald except for a few reddish hairs plastered over it and he had cheeks the color of raw beefsteak.

"Confidentially, Mr. Archer," I heard him say, "this is the worst thing that ever happened to me."

He glared at Uncle Percy but he was very respectful for all his jerky talk.

"Yes, sir, the worst. I had everything figgered out, see? Read everything on your Riel rebellion—Duck Lake, Cut Knife Creek,

Batoche—everything. A natural for fillum—tremenjous."

He began to lunge back and forth across the room, waving a cigar and pinching his flat nose as if to stretch it.

"Sure, I could do it cheaper in Hollywood but I wanted the real background, the feel of it—Mounted Police, half-breeds, Indians—no slapstick, no fake—a Canadian saga—authentic. And what happens?"

Uncle Percy listened from behind the desk, tapping it with his fingers.

"It's all going fine, see, a great cast—three stars—a galaxy, by God—costumes, properties, the works. And we get here and my heavy reports sick—indisposed. Indisposed? Drunk as a skunk in that lousy Majestic joint. Perfect, he was, for Riel. But he won't be sober for a week, maybe a month, that lush. Back he goes to Hollywood, and no pay either."

"I understand," said Uncle Percy.

"No—beg pardon—you don't. Confidentially, this outfit costs three grand a day—my money, see? I tell you, Mr. Archer, I'm just about ready to fold it, cut the losses but then I get a notion. That's where you come in."

"I come in?"

Garrett leaned over the desk, suddenly grinning and winking, his cigar thrust at Uncle Percy.

"There's a fella from the paper—name of Brindle or something like that—he's interviewing me—says you used to be on the stage, legitimate stuff, in London, he says. Right?"

"Only small parts," said Uncle Percy. "As a youngster, you know. With Irving."

"What! You mean *the* Irving? *Henry* Irving?"

"Well, yes. I understudied him for a while. Played Hamlet twice when he caught cold in Manchester. But a poor show I made of it."

Garrett blew out his scarlet cheeks.

"I'll be damned! Irving! Hamlet! Why, you could *easy* play Riel—nothing to it—perfect."

"With my accent? Hardly. He was French and Indian."

72

"Doesn't matter—no accent on fillum, no sound—just subtitles and we fix 'em to suit. Yes sir, perfect."

"But Riel was a traitor. They hanged him. I shouldn't like..."

"Don't worry. There'll be no hanging, no politics—just clean entertainment, see? Romance."

Garrett aimed the cigar at his shiny head. "In here, Mr. Archer—the story line—always in here. Keep it open, flexible—never freeze it—put it together, make it fit after we fillum. That's my method."

"But really, you know...."

"Just leave it to me, Mr. Archer. And wait till you meet my two stars—great, both of 'em—tremenjous. And you won't even ride a horse in the battle scene. I'll use a double, a stunt man—no danger."

Uncle Percy gave him a faint smile. "I'm rather used to horses. Did a spot of riding in South Africa, the cavalry. But I was only a lieutenant, young and green."

Garrett's mouth opened wide.

"This beats all! With Irving! And the cavalry! Then you'll have to do it—any pay you want—money no object. With my two stars it's a lead-pipe cinch."

"I don't quite see," Uncle Percy muttered. "Well, perhaps..."

He was twirling the points of his mustache and I knew the signs. He'd do it.

"Good, good, bully," cried Garrett. "We'll set up camp today—hire locals for the mob scenes—start rehearsal tomorrow."

So they did, on the range south of Hogarth's spread a couple of miles from town. When I rode there after school I saw that Garrett had wasted no time.

Three tents stood near the crumbling log cabin where us kids used to play outlaw, and inside, a fat Chinese cook had pots boiling on a camp stove. A crew of roustabouts were pegging down some fake canvas teepees and, behind them, in the poplar grove, a bunch of Hogarth's ranch hands and some Indians from the Quintlam Reserve seemed to be waiting on their cayuses for something, but I couldn't make out what.

Garrett sprawled on a folding chair beside two cameras on wooden legs and shouted directions through a megaphone. His fancy suit had been changed for a pink shirt, riding pants, high boots, and brown sombrero.

A scruffy little man, no taller than me, fiddled with the cameras and squinted through their sights, his muddy face crumpled and twitching. He wore his cap back to front and a dead cigarette butt dangled from his lips. Garrett called him Wilf. He only twitched and snarled, saying nothing.

Back of the director's chair some folks from town were watching his outfit at work and I edged close to Dandy Ryan's Reo. He had Hogarth, Brindle and Foster with him. Paul Jessup arrived on his bicycle and scribbled in a notebook. The *Echo*'s reporter looked serious.

"Quiet, please," Garrett called over his shoulder. "Today's just rehearsal, see? A few test shots to get the feel of it, that's all."

He swung his megaphone at the Indians in the poplar grove.

"First the medicine dance. Come on, then, Sitting Bull, like I showed you—straight ahead, see, and stop halfway."

I could scarcely believe it when Chief Skookum Barnabas walked out of the poplars in a headdress of feathers, a striped blanket and fringed leggings. He was holding a carved pipe, about three feet long, and looked mighty uncomfortable. As he came closer I saw that his row of silver teeth had been blacked out and dark lines painted around his single good eye and the empty one.

About a dozen Indians followed him, mostly naked, their skin oily and shining, feathers stuck in their hair, faces smeared with paint. They carried bows and arrows and some clumsy guns— from Hollywood, I guessed.

"Now sit down, Chief," Garrett shouted. "On that rock there. And start smoking. Roll it, Wilf."

Wilf snarled but kept turning the crank of the camera.

Barnabas sat on the rock and sucked his pipe, blowing smoke out of his mouth.

"You've just killed Custer," said Garrett. "You're on your way to

74

fight for Riel, see, and kill more white men. You're praying to the Great Spirit up in the sky. Get it?"

Barnabas didn't seem to get it very well but his good eye stared at the sky.

"And start talking. Say something. Say anything."

"It's a nice day," said Barnabas. "It's sure a nice day."

He spat on the ground. "This pipe tastes like hell."

"Fine," cried Garrett. "Now you boys dance around him. Go ahead, dance."

The Indians began to circle Barnabas, jumping up and down, waving their bows and guns and howling.

"Faster! Faster!" Garrett shouted.

They danced faster and howled louder but some of them were laughing.

"Not bad for a first take," said Garrett. "Cut it, Wilf."

Jessup had stopped scribbling and glowered at me through his thick spectacles.

"It's all wrong," he grumbled. "Sitting Bull wasn't near Riel, only in Alberta, and years before the rebellion. Grotesque, a serious distortion of history."

Garrett had overheard Jessup and rounded on him.

"You there, mind your own business."

"But the facts," said Jessup. "The history."

"I'm not making history, see, I'm making drama. The public where I come from never heard of Riel but they know Sitting Bull, they want him in and, by God, he will be. Shut up, young fella, or I'll run you off the set."

Garrett turned back to the camera. Jessup put the notebook in his pocket and pedaled away on the bicycle, still grumbling.

"That'll teach the son of a bitch," Dandy grunted from the Reo.

"He's fired," said Brindle.

"Till tomorrow," Hogarth chuckled.

Garrett aimed his megaphone at the tents. "Next, a shot of Riel. Are you ready, Mr. Archer?"

I hadn't seen Uncle Percy yet and when he came out of the

biggest tent I couldn't recognize his face under a curly black wig and square beard. He was dressed in a buckskin coat, leather pants and beaded moccasins. A silver cross hung around his neck and a revolver was stuck in his belt. I tried not to giggle.

"Ready," he said. "Quite ready."

One of the roustabouts led Hogarth's bay stallion from the trees and Uncle Percy mounted lightly into the saddle. I knew that horse, a tall, lean, nervous brute with flaring nostrils and wild eyes. He'd always frightened me, but not Uncle Percy.

"Ride this way," said Garrett. "Ride slow. And don't look at the camera. Roll it. Wilf."

The stallion trembled and shied but Uncle Percy reined him in and looked past the camera, a hand shading his eyes against the sun.

"Good, good, Mr. Archer! Now come a little further. Quick, Wilf, a close-up."

Wilf moved over to the second camera and kept cranking it till Uncle Percy stopped a few feet off.

"Riel to the life! Now start talking. You're brooding, see, on the wrongs of your people—revenge, rebellion—all that. Say anything, anything."

Uncle Percy stared across the range and I guess he said the first thing he could think of.

"To be or not to be, that is the question. Whether 'tis nobler in the mind..."

Garrett sprang out of his chair. "Wonderful! But now change the mood. You're planning war, see, you're out for blood—hate, passion, let it all out."

Uncle Percy shook a clenched fist at the sky and rose in his stirrups. His voice rose, too.

"Once more unto the breach, dear friends, once more or close up the wall with our English dead..."

"Cut it, Wilf. That's passion, that's terrific. Shakespeare even!"

"If that's Riel" Dandy snickered, "I'm the Duke of Kakiak."

"If that's Percy," said Hogarth, "he needs a shave and a hair-

76

cut."

In all the fuss I hadn't noticed Aunt Minerva drive up to the edge of the crowd in her new dog-cart behind the chestnut colt with Aunt Lizzie under a green parasol. They were beside me before I could escape.

"What's going on, boy?" Aunt Minerva demanded.

"They're rehearsing," I said. "For the movie."

"Where's your uncle?"

I pointed to the stallion.

"That dreadful man in whiskers? My land!"

"He's made up for Riel."

"Made up for a fool. Ha! I'll make him up when he gets home. Riel indeed! Fiddlesticks."

"Disgusting," Aunt Lizzie whimpered.

Aunt Minerva tickled the colt with her whip and drove away. But I knew Uncle Percy's sweet talk would cool her down.

Luckily he didn't see her and now he swung out of the saddle.

Garrett seized his hand. "Perfect, perfect, Mr. Archer. No need for another shot. Yeah, authentic."

"Adequate, I hope," Uncle Percy murmured. "But I'm a bit rusty, you know. What next?"

"Next, the other stars run through a clinch."

"A clinch?"

"Just the old routine—boy meets girl. This cop, Mounted Police of course—he saves her from Riel in the rebellion—love interest—happy ending. It's all in here."

Garrett tapped his sweaty forehead and shouted through the megaphone again.

"Lorraine—Brand—are you ready?"

"In a minute," a woman's voice answered from one of the tents.

"Always late," the Director growled. "But the hottest property on fillum."

"I haven't met the lady yet," said Uncle Percy as he stripped off his wig.

"Lady! Huh, found. her slinging hash in the Grand Central

Station—Molly Flanagan she was—practically illiterate—but I saw right away she had it."

"Had it?"

"You bet—sex to burn—box office—surefire. So I give her a French name—Gabrielle Lorraine. The public goes for that foreign stuff—glamor, romance, see? And I sign her and put her on every screen in America."

"Remarkable," said Uncle Percy.

"Yeah, and top pay, a hundred a week. But do I get any thanks from that little tramp? No, sir. Head's swelled too big for her britches."

"Remarkable."

"She can't act for sour apples but look at her face—look at the curves—look at those boobs! Any red-blooded American wants to sleep with her and I wouldn't mind, myself. But she's damned choosey."

"And Mr. Brand?"

"Another hot property, just as hot as Gaby. Found him in Omaha tending bar—Sam Hincks, farm boy, corn-fed, dumb—but he had it. So I call him Beverly Brand—put him and Gaby together—six fillums already—smash hits, all of 'em."

"Remarkable."

"Women dote on him, every man jealous. Sex and jealousy—you can't beat that combination. They hate each other but he's perfect for the cop. Here's Gaby."

When Miss Lorraine came out of the tent I saw what the director meant. Plenty of curves showed through her tight purple blouse. A leather skirt ended just above her knees and cowboy boots. Her face and two braids of golden hair were like the pictures of the Virgin Mary in my Sunday school book. But I thought her cheeks had been painted too much.

Brand followed her, in a stiff Stetson hat, a red coat and striped riding pants. He looked exactly like the Mounties I'd seen in Kamloops. His curly hair was as golden as Lorraine's but the thin line of his mustache was almost black.

78

They stood in front of the camera, both sulky.

"We'll just do a quick run through," Garrett told them "The old clinch. But we can use it in the last fade-out if it works. Close up, Wilf. And keep those boobs in the frame."

"Christ," said Lorraine, "dontcha ever get a new idear?"

"Enough of that," the director snapped. "Let's go."

Wilf began to crank the camera.

Brand wrapped his arms around Lorraine and they grinned at each other, baring their white teeth.

Garrett spat out his cigar.

"Lousy, just lousy! Put some life in it. Look in her eyes. Emote, godammit!"

Lorraine's long eyelashes fluttered and so did Brand's as he hugged her tight.

"Start talking."

Lorraine sighed, kind of soft and dreamy.

"You bin eatin' onions again."

"And you're still on gin," Brand murmured but he kept grinning.

"Closer, closer!" Garrett bawled. "Now the kiss."

Brand pressed his lips down hard on Lorraine's and her hand stroked his golden curls.

"Not bad," said Garrett. "Cut it, Wilf. Might do for a fade-out, at that."

After the stars had gone back to their tent Garrett turned to Uncle Percy.

"Not much like Shakespeare, eh? But fillum's different."

"Of course. Yes remarkable."

Garrett pinched his nose and seemed to be in deep thought.

"Yeah, but I've got a better story line. Just hit me, sudden, in here—terrific. She's not a white girl, see, she's half Indian, half French—Riel's daughter! The cop falls for her—love against duty—God, what a twist! Put a black wig on her—darken her skin—perfect!"

Uncle Percy scratched his fake beard.

"I don't quite understand..."

"You will, you will! The cop shoots you in the battle—you fall dead—he grabs the girl off her horse—saves her from the rebellion—clinch and fade-out. It's a natural."

"But they hanged Riel."

"What of it? The American public don't know and they want a happy ending, see."

Uncle Percy gaped at him.

"Happy ending? The daughter takes the man who killed her father? Well, really..."

"Oh, she'll get over it—love conquers all—surefire stuff—I'll work out the details in here—keep it flexible till it's all on fillum—leave everything to me."

They left everything to Garrett for the next three days but I couldn't watch him work out the details because the summer exams kept me late at school.

When I rode to the movie camp on Saturday most of the scenes had been finished. Now Barnabas and the Indians were galloping into the poplar grove and out again, shooting arrows and whooping. About a dozen of Hogarth's ranch hands, in Mountie uniforms, followed them, firing blank cartridges from their revolvers while Garrett yelled through his megaphone and Wilf cranked the camera. Uncle Percy stood beside the director in his ordinary clothes, without the wig and beard.

It was quite a while before Garrett seemed to be satisfied and Wilf stopped cranking. The Indians and the Mounties hustled around the log cabin and the Chinaman fed them stew.

"On fillum," Garrett told Uncle Percy, "they'll look like hundreds, thousands. But tomorrow's different. You never know what'll go wrong in a battle. Mob scenes—they're always risky. And Gaby and Brand, scared to death, the bastards."

Next morning early a crowd from town came out to watch the battle scene. Ryan brought Hogarth, Brindle and Foster in the Reo. Jessup had appeared with bicycle and notebook.

Garrett raised his megaphone.

"Ladies and gentlemen, welcome to this saga of the great

rebellion. But stand back, please, so nobody gets hurt. Thank you."

His three stars were beside him and the cameras for final instructions, I guessed.

Uncle Percy, again in wig and beard, sat on the nervous bay stallion and patted his neck, gentling him.

A quiet little roan had been chosen for Lorraine. She wore a black wig, too, with long braids, her face darkened but still pretty.

Brand, on a clumsy old pinto, was decked out in his red coat and striped pants and he sweated through his grease paint.

Garrett looked up at Uncle Percy.

"I wish you'd let me use a double, Mr. Archer. No one's going to see the difference on fillum."

"We've been over that before," said Uncle Percy.

"Well, if you say so. But I don't like it."

"Christ, you think I do?" Lorraine muttered.

"It's a bitch," said Brand. "Crazy."

The Indians and the ranch hands waited beyond the poplar grove on their cayuses. The director glanced at them and shook his head.

"Rehearsed and rehearsed, over and over, but you never know."

He turned back to the stars.

"You've got it, eh? The breeds running away—Riel and Gaby a little behind—full gallop. Then comes the cops—Brand in front— catches up—drags Gaby out of the saddle and shoots Riel—he falls off, dead. That's dangerous, Mr. Archer. We could still use a double."

"I'll manage," said Uncle Percy. "It's an old trick in the cavalry."

"I don't like it, but let's go. You start when I wave, see. Don't act, just ride, ride like hell straight past the camera. You ready, Wilf?"

Wilf snarled. The stars rode over to the poplar bluff. Garrett tried to light a cigar but the wind blew out the match. No sound came from the crowd.

Garrett waved a white handkerchief.

"Roll it, Wilf."

After that everything happened so fast that I saw only a whirl of horses through the dust, Barnabas in his streaming feathers ahead of the Indians, a blur of buckskin and naked bodies, flashes of red, Uncle Percy and Lorraine riding neck and neck, Brand close behind, waving a revolver.

"Grab her!" the director bawled. "Shoot him and grab her! Oh, Jesus..."

Brand caught up with the little roan mare and stretched out his arm to Lorraine. The mare stumbled and Lorraine was falling from the saddle. But she didn't fall.

Uncle Percy grabbed her around the waist and held her, wriggling and screaming. Brand lay on the ground. The Indians and Mounties passed him but I couldn't see much in all the dust.

Garrett had collapsed through his canvas chair. The crowd was yelling and I was yelling, too. Wilf still cranked the camera.

That night Uncle Percy came home with his left arm in a sling. Doc Halleck had fixed it and told him that only a small bone was broken in the wrist and would soon mend.

"Serves you right, you old fool," said Aunt Minerva. "At your age!"

I could tell she was upset all the same, her hand shaking as she poured a glass of brandy. Uncle Percy gulped it and sat down on the sofa. She poured another glass.

"I warned you but no, you wouldn't listen."

"Oh, to think of it!" Aunt Lizzie whimpered. "That awful American."

But when Garrett knocked at the door Aunt Minerva let him in without a word and left him with Uncle Percy in the parlor. From the kitchen I saw the blue lump on the director's shiny head and sticking plaster on both cheeks.

"Terrible," he began. "Terrible. I should have used a double."

"It's nothing," said Uncle Percy. "But it spoils your picture."

"No, no! A few more shots and it'll be better than ever. Got it all in here and the battle on fillum—terrific."

"I don't understand..."

"You will, you will, Riel saves the girl, see—gives her back to the

82

cop—a father's love and all that—rides into the sunset—nobody stops him—rebellion's finished. Perfect!"

"Riel was hanged, you know."

"Not on fillum. Who'd hang a hero? But that's detail—I'll work it out all right—a happy ending—a saga by God—pure Canada, authentic."

Uncle Percy shrugged.

"Oh well," he said.

Next day Wilf made a long shot of him on the stallion riding away from the camera, his wrist still bandaged but the sun hadn't begun to set in the afternoon sky.

There was no movie theatre in Emerald Vale yet so we never got to see the great director's saga. But months later Jessup saw the show in Spokane and told me it was a serious distortion of history.

The Love Affair

Dandy Ryan fell dead of a heart attack in Victoria before he could make his first speech in the Legislature. They shipped him home on the train from Vancouver but it was held up by a snowslide in the Fraser Canyon and Lem Brady, the station agent, said it wouldn't get to Emerald Vale till morning at earliest. No one remembered a cold snap like this—forty below, nearly two feet of snow on the ground, with a north wind that seemed to peel the skin off my face.

It was still dark when Uncle Percy and I harnessed the chestnut colt and drove to the station in the cutter. He took me along to help him and the others with the coffin. We found Hogarth and Brindle sitting around the drum stove in Lem's office. Presently I saw Tex drive a freight sled up to the platform and cover his team of Clydesdales with blankets. He came stamping into the room to get the snow off his boots.

"I call that cold," he grumbled.

The others said nothing but let him stand close to the stove. Tiny icicles hanging from his beard began to melt and drip.

We waited for the train's whistle but all we heard was the rattle of the telegraph ticker. Brady hunched over it, listening, a wet cigarette in his mouth.

"She's passed the junction," he said at last and soon we heard the whistle. It was just getting light when the train pulled up to the platform, belching smoke and steam.

The double doors of the baggage car swung open and a couple of brakemen slid the coffin out. It was made of black, shiny wood with two brass handles on each side. We took hold of them and lifted the coffin down. It felt mighty heavy as we lugged it to the freight shed. Dandy had always been fat.

"You stay with Tex," Uncle Percy told me. "He may need you. We'll go on ahead."

The three men got into the cutter and drove off, the colt's strap of bells jingling, his breath trailing behind. I climbed to the seat beside Tex and he spread the horse blankets over our knees.

"Giddup thar," he said and slapped the reins on the Clydesdales' backs. They strained into their collars, the sled began to move and the runners made a swishing sound on the packed snow.

After a while I asked Tex where he was taking the coffin.

"You'll see," he grunted.

Soon he turned off the main road and I saw that we were going to Miss Stella's big square house. Often I'd brought letters and parcels there from town and she always gave me a quarter for the errand, once a dollar bill. I was never inside the house but I knew Miss Stella's business. The whole town knew it, even the kids in school. Everybody knew, too, that she'd sent the other women away when she took up with Dandy. They'd been living together for the last year but nobody talked much about it any more.

Tex stopped his team at the door.

"Hold the reins," he said, "and don't look, mind."

I gripped the reins in my mitts and he clambered stiffly from the sled. Over my shoulder I saw him push up the lid of the coffin but I couldn't see Dandy.

The door opened and Miss Stella came out, a brown fur coat wrapped around her nightdress, her legs bare above her clumsy gumboots. She was a big woman, taller than Dandy and a lot younger, not pretty but handsome, I guess, ruddy and strong. Now

86

she looked old, her cheeks pale, dark smudges under her eyes.

"Easy, Stella," Tex muttered. "Take it easy."

When I glanced back again she was leaning over the coffin and I expected her to cry. But she didn't.

"Easy now," said Tex.

Then I saw her pull a ring off her finger and drop it into the coffin. After that I watched the horses and felt like crying, myself.

It seemed a long time before Miss Stella turned away and the door of the house closed behind her. She hadn't said a word.

Tex folded down the lid of the coffin and climbed to the seat and we headed for town. I hadn't cried but I wondered what was going to happen to Miss Stella alone in that big house. Tex must have been wondering, too.

"It's tough on her," he said. "She was fond of him, mighty fond. You'll know better when you're growed."

He said no more till the horses stopped in the lane back of Ed Wilby's furniture store. There was no undertaker in Emerald Vale and Wilby buried dead people as a sideline, dressed for the funerals in a tailcoat and silk hat. Now he was standing on the steps with Uncle Percy, Brindle, Hogarth and Doc Foster. Under a bushy fur hat his scrawny little face was puckered and red from the cold.

"I done what you wanted," said Tex.

"How'd she take it?" Brindle asked.

"Pretty good, but it's tough on her. Dandy looked fine, all slicked up like he was sleepin' peaceful."

"Bring him in then," said Wilby. "Quick, I'm froze."

They lifted the coffin off the sled and carried it into the store and laid it on a long wooden bench.

"He'll be all right there till we get the grave dug out," Wilby told them. "Ground's solid three feet deep and they're blastin' it. Funeral's Monday if the snow let's up. It's a bugger."

That afternoon I did my Saturday chores tidying Uncle Percy's office and fixing wood and coal for the stove. He sat at his desk in the front room, talking to his friends.

"Dandy must of left quite a pile," Hogarth was saying. "The

hotel's a gold mine."

Uncle Percy took some papers from his desk.

"Here's the will. He made it before he left town and I notarized it. We're all joint executors."

"He never told me," said Brindle.

"No, it was in confidence. But of course no longer. He left everything to Miss Stella—the Majestic, cash, even the motor car."

Brindle squirmed in his chair.

"What about the *Echo*?"

Uncle Percy smiled and glanced down at the papers.

"He left his shares in the *Echo* to his friend and associate, Michael Brindle Esquire in token of gratitude and esteem. So reads the will. I wrote it."

Brindle's pasty cheeks were trembling. He tried to speak but no words came out.

Hogarth patted his shoulder.

"You earned it, Mike. You made the *Echo*. And Miss Stella's rich. Christ, he should of married her."

"Yes, and I'm sure he would have except for politics," said Uncle Percy. "It wouldn't do, you know, so long as he was in the Legislature. But that was their own business, only theirs. It was a . . . a love affair."

"I wisht we hadn't run him," Hogarth grunted.

"Might still be alive," said Foster.

I heard a pounding on the front door and the new preacher from England stumbled into the office, wheezing and panting—a dumpy, beefy little man, his face lined with crimson veins. On a sign in front of the church he was called the Reverend Arthur Gregg, D.D., Oxon, but the kids at Sunday school called him Old Drippy because a bead of moisture always seemed to be hanging from his swollen, purple nose.

Now he rubbed a woollen mitt against it and unwrapped his long, black scarf.

"Gentlemen," he began in his snuffling English voice, "pardon this intrusion but there is—ah—a matter of which—ah—I am compelled to speak."

"Indeed?" said Uncle Percy.

"Yes a matter of some—ah—delicacy. It has come to my knowledge—ah—that a certain woman, a notorious woman I may say, will attend the funeral of the late—ah—Mr. Ryan. Impossible, gentlemen, quite impossible, as you must agree."

"Like hell we do!" Brindle spluttered.

Gregg ignored him.

"I find," he went on, "that—ah—Mr. Ryan was not a member of our congregation or even—ah—a regular attendant. However..."

Brindle jumped up from his chair.

"But he gave the land for the church didn't he and money to help build it."

"That may be. I do not know," Gregg snuffled. "But I cannot permit the woman to attend. It would not be—ah, fitting."

Uncle Percy pounded his desk.

"What! You a Christian minister and hurl the first stone?"

"If she don't come," Hogarth shouted, "Dandy won't come, nobody'll come. We'll take him somewheres else and be damned to you and your bloody church!"

Gregg rubbed his nose again.

"I should have thought that—ah—the female in question..."

Brindle cut him short.

"No matter what you thought! She was his friend. And ours, too."

"Who are you, who are we to judge them?" said Uncle Percy. "Enough, sir, enough."

Gregg opened his mouth to say something but closed it and slowly wrapped the scarf around his neck.

"Very well then," he mumbled. "So be it if that's the—ah—custom of the country. You gentlemen must take the responsibility. I cannot."

He turned and waddled out the door.

Hogarth watched him through the window.

"The bastard," he growled. "The sneakin' jeeslin' bastard!"

"Indeed," said Uncle Percy. "Is he not?"

That night, at supper, I could tell that Uncle Percy was worried. He hardly touched his food.

Aunt Minerva saw it, too.

"What's wrong with you?" she demanded.

"Nothing, my dear, nothing. Except..."

"I know. It's the funeral. Well, you can go but not me. I never liked that man. And his women."

"One woman, only one. And you must go. The look of the thing. Dandy was my friend."

"Your friend, not mine."

"A simple fellow, a rough diamond but good-hearted, generous, honest. He meant no harm and faithful to her, in his fashion."

"That woman? Will she be there?"

"She will. Why not? Even Gregg understands."

"He does, eh? He would, the old fool."

Aunt Lizzy sniffled.

"Disgusting."

The argument was still going on when Marie cleared away the dishes. Gradually Aunt Minerva backed down.

"If I go," she said, "don't expect me to speak to the woman."

"No, no, my dear. Of course not."

"I'm not going," said Aunt Lizzy." I never enjoy funerals."

But she agreed to stay home and fix sandwiches for the pall-bearers and the preacher and a few of Dandy's friends after they'd buried him. Marie promised to bake a seedcake.

"A glass of sherry, perhaps, a sip of hot rum," Uncle Percy suggested. "They'll all be chilled to the bone."

"Tea and coffee, no liquor," said Aunt Minerva. But in the end she backed down again, admitting that the weather was cold. The thermometer outside the kitchen door had dropped below forty by bedtime.

On Monday afternoon Uncle Percy and I harnessed the colt but without his string of bells. Aunt Minerva put a couple of hot bricks, wrapped in flannel, on the floor of the cutter. We tucked the buffalo

90

skin around us and drove to the church.

Horses and empty sleighs lined the street. The coffin lay on the freight sled and Tex stood holding the Clydesdales' halters. Brindle, Hogarth and Foster waited beside the sled with Wilby. Paul Jessup was behind them, scribbling in his notebook.

"You two go inside," Uncle Percy whispered to Aunt Minerva.

We went in and found the church packed. Most of the people were strangers to me but in the back row I saw Miss Stella in her brown fur coat and hat. She was looking straight ahead as if she didn't see anybody, all the color drained out of her face. Skookum Barnabas and some Indians from Quintlam in their checked mackinaws filled the rest of the row and they looked straight ahead, too.

Aunt Minerva and I were led to the front pew and we sat down close to the pulpit and a huge wreath of flowers from the Kamloops greenhouse.

Gregg was standing by the pulpit in a white surplice over a long black robe. The heat of the drum stove in the corner seemed to have deepened the purple of his cheeks and nose.

The stove smoked. The flowers gave out a sickly smell. I started to sweat and fidget. But it was a nice little church, built only a year ago. Its wooden beams and ceiling shone with varnish and the sun lit up the stained glass windows.

Aunt Minerva nudged me.

"Stop wriggling, boy, and sit still. That woman—is she here?"

"In the back row," I said. "With the Indians."

Just then everybody stood up and a cold draft blew through the church door. Uncle Percy, Hogarth, Brindle and Foster carried in the coffin, all of them panting as they laid it in front of the altar.

At a nod from Wilby they slid into the pew next to Aunt Minerva and me.

I didn't pay much attention to the service, thinking of Dandy in that big box and Miss Stella in the back row.

Gregg rubbed a handkerchief against his nose and opened a bible. Snuffling and wheezing, he read some verses and we knelt down while he mumbled a prayer. When he'd finished, with a hoarse "amen" we stood up.

A man with a shriveled yellow face began to work the organ pedals under his feet. I recognized the hymn from Sunday school and Aunt Minerva and I sang "Fight the Good Fight" but Uncle Percy kept his mouth closed tight. His mind must have been on something else. I wondered about it till Gregg coughed and dabbed the handkerchief against his nose again.

"In this congregation," he said, "it is fitting and appropriate that Mr. Archer, an old friend of our—ah—departed brother should pay a tribute to—ah—his memory."

Uncle Percy stepped into the middle of the aisle, bowed to the altar and turned to the congregation. He looked fine in his high white collar and tailcoat, but nervous. His hands, under the starched cuffs, were shaking.

Afterwards everybody said it was a good speech but I can remember only the last words.

"...he came as a stranger to this land and served it faithfully and well as a staunch Canadian, a loyal British subject. Our debt to him is heavy and so are our hearts. We say farewell to a kindly, generous man whose human failings were swallowed up in charity that knew no limit and left no enemies."

When Uncle Percy sat down his eyes were brimming. Aunt Minerva patted his hand. I felt a little choked, myself. Dandy had always been kind to me.

Gregg bowed his head and mumbled another prayer. The wizened man pumped the organ and the four pallbearers lifted the coffin by its brass handles and carried it to the freight sled.

Aunt Minerva and I followed the congregation outside. Tex slumped in the driver's seat, holding a tight rein on the Clydesdales. Uncle Percy was standing bare-headed among a cluster of his friends and Barnabas was shaking his hand.

"Tillicum," the Chief said, "hiyu tillicum, that Dandy."

Foster sat in his red sleigh, Wilby and Brindle with him. But I couldn't see Hogarth and Miss Stella and guessed he'd taken her home.

Everybody waited for Gregg. Now he waddled down the steps in his black overcoat and a scarf wrapped around a flimsy English cap, almost hiding his face. I was surprised to see him climb up beside Tex on the driver's seat. Tex clucked to the horses and they moved off.

"Put your hat on Percy," said Aunt Minerva, "or you'll catch pneumonia, likely."

He put on his fur hat and the three of us got into the cutter. Even with the buffalo robe it was a freezing cold drive to the graveyard about two miles from town. Foster's sleigh was ahead of us, ours and maybe a dozen others behind.

On the hill across the river Tex had brought the freight sled to the edge of an oblong hole and a heap of frozen clay. Four men, strangers to me, leaned on their shovels looking into the hole. Gregg stood at one end and shivered. Wilby, Brindle and Foster were beside the sled and looked at the coffin. More sleighs came up the hill, then Barnabas and his Indians on their cayuses. No one spoke in the circle around the grave.

Uncle Percy took Aunt Minerva's arm and helped her to the side opposite the sled and I moved back of them, feeling cold and kind of foolish to be there at all.

"That woman," Aunt Minerva whispered, "she didn't come."

"No, my dear," said Uncle Percy, "and just as well."

Wilby beckoned to the men behind the heap of clay. They brought ropes and looped them under the coffin. Gregg was taking a small book from his pocket when I saw Hogarth's sleigh at the outer rim of the circle. Miss Stella was with him.

Hogarth put his arm around her waist as they stumbled through the snow.

"The woman!" Aunt Minerva whispered.

"Oh God!" said Uncle Percy.

But they stepped aside to make room for Miss Stella at the end of the hole. She didn't seem to notice them. Her eyes were fixed on the coffin.

"All right, boys," said Wilby.

The four men tugged at the ropes and eased the coffin off the sled until it hung between them above the hole.

Gregg started to read from his book. Miss Stella's eyes never left the coffin and they were dry. Aunt Minerva watched her sideways with a queer look I hadn't seen before.

The men slowly loosened the ropes and the coffin disappeared.

"Steady there," said Wilby.

"Ashes to ashes, dust to dust," Gregg snuffled. He looked around him for a moment and picked up a handful of snow and tossed it into the hole. The coffin hit the hard earth at the bottom with a thud and the men dropped the ropes.

It was only then that tears streamed down Miss Stella's cheeks. She sank to her knees, limp all over. But as she fell Aunt Minerva's arms were around her.

"Quick, Percy! She's fainted."

Together they lifted Miss Stella up. Her eyes were closed and she was gasping like she would choke.

"I'll take her home," said Hogarth.

"No, we will," said Aunt Minerva. "And hurry."

Between them, Uncle Percy and Hogarth carried Miss Stella to our cutter. Aunt Minerva covered her with the buffalo robe and sat beside her. Uncle Percy picked up the reins, the colt snorted and went off at a trot.

Hogarth was half frowning and half smiling as he watched them go.

"Well, I'll be God-damned," he said.

We walked back to the grave. The men with the shovels were throwing chunks of clay that thumped on the coffin. Tex hadn't moved from the freight sled and the Clydesdales didn't move, either, but their heads were drooping. Wilby and Gregg huddled with Brindle in Foster's sleigh under a blanket. The rest of the sleighs were gone.

"That Minerva!" Brindle muttered. "Christ, who'd of thought..."

"Come, on," said Foster. "It's gettin' dark."

94

Hogarth offered me a lift to town but I said I'd ride with Tex. The others drove away.

It was pitch dark and snowing again when Tex and I got to the livery stable. He boiled up some coffee in the harness room and I rubbed down the Clydesdales and fed them hay and oats. We drank the bitter coffee and nibbled some stale crackers beside the stove. The old man was silent for a long time.

"Too bad," he said at last, "Dandy couldn't see them take her home. It would've suited him fine, jest fine. He was fond of her."

I wondered about Miss Stella alone in that big square house but Tex said Hogarth would see she was all right.

"He's there already, I reckon."

All the same, I was still wondering as I trudged to our house in the driving snow and found Marie in the kitchen, washing dishes at the sink.

"*Mon Dieu!*" she cried. "You're freezed."

I tucked into the leavings of the sandwiches and the seedcake on the table.

"Where's everybody?" I asked.

"Oh that *pauvre femme!*" said Marie. "She was so sick and they put her in bed upstairs."

I stopped eating.

"Who? You mean Miss Stella?"

"*Oui*, and the doctor came and gave her pills to sleep. *Quel jour!*"

Then Marie began to giggle.

"The men, they ate everything up and that preacher fella he was boozy."

I hadn't got my mind around the news when Uncle Percy came downstairs in his dressing gown and slippers. He took a bottle from the cupboard and filled a tumbler with sherry. The day, I guessed, had been pretty hard on him.

He gulped down the sherry and seemed to notice me for the first time.

"My boy," he said, "your aunt is a remarkable woman. Remarkable. And don't you ever forget it."

A Great Day

The *Echo* said it would be the greatest day in the history of Emerald Vale when Robert Borden turned on the first electric lights. I thought, myself, that Uncle Percy had written the editorial. The style was too fancy for Brindle.

"By a propitious conjunction of events the Leader of His Majesty's Loyal Opposition and the future Prime Minister, visiting our city in the course of his triumphant election tour, will inaugurate the electrical age and, in this symbolic act, will illuminate the fatal madness of Reciprocity."

The whole town talked about the election campaign in the spring of 1911 but all I knew about Reciprocity was that it would ruin Canada. Uncle Percy said so at dinner every night.

"Just politics, nothing serious," Jessup told me. "Another of Laurier's slippery tricks. And it'll work again. The Tories can't beat the old shyster."

Jessup was against electricity, too.

"They'll never get it going before Borden comes," he said. "The thing's preposterous, a waste of money."

The Emerald Vale Light and Power Corporation Inc. didn't seem to be worried and went ahead with its plans. Hogarth was President, Uncle Percy, Treasurer, and Brindle and Foster, Directors. Now and then I listened to them arguing in the front office when I fixed wood for the stove in the back.

But I couldn't make out much about their Corporation, only that all of them had bought shares. Uncle Percy must have bought a heap because he warned Aunt Minerva to go easy on expenses in the house till his quarterly cheque came from England.

Miss Stella, I gathered, was the biggest shareholder. She had sold her house and moved into the Majestic and done it all over from top to bottom with plaster and paint and a lot of new furniture. Even the crimson Reo was repainted and Hogarth taught her to drive it. A tinted photograph of Dandy, two feet square, hung in the lobby and people said his hotel was making more money than ever.

It set a good table with the best meat from Fire Chief Ben Stott's butcher shop but the meals were high at fifty cents. Miss Stella kept a close watch on the Chinese cook, Lee Gung, in the kitchen, and her three housemaids. If I ran errands for her on Saturdays she always gave me a dollar and all the pie I could eat.

"You're too thin," she'd say. "Boys need grub. You want to grow up a skinny malink and die young? Eat, boy, eat."

I guess Dandy had made Miss Stella richer than anyone in Emerald Vale but her name wasn't listed with the other shareholders in the *Echo*.

"It's just her reputation," I heard Uncle Percy tell the Directors. "The town wouldn't understand. Unfair, but there it is."

"And she won't talk," said Hogarth. "You can trust her."

I didn't talk either. By now I felt mean listening at all and I'd liked Miss Stella long before Dandy's funeral.

"She's gettin' over Dandy pretty good," said Foster.

Hogarth shook his head. "No, she'll never."

I wondered about that. Sometimes I thought Miss Stella had almost forgotten Dandy. The color was back in her cheeks again, she bustled around the hotel with her eye on everything, she joshed with the commercial travelers at the desk, she emptied the cash at night and put the money in the iron safe under Dandy's picture and she was the first up in the morning.

But sometimes her face had that same frozen look that I'd seen when Tex opened the coffin at her house. I wondered.

The Directors of the Corporation, I could see, had other things on their minds. They needed oodles of money for the electric plant and they were selling shares all over town, even some in Kamloops and the Okanagan. Most of the stores in Emerald Vale contracted to buy electricity and Miss Stella was having a big sign made in Vancouver to hang in front of the hotel with the word "Majestic" spelled out in light bulbs. The *Echo* said that "every household will soon enjoy this miracle of science."

Near the end of March I found a stranger in Uncle Percy's office talking to the Directors—an odd-looking man of middle age, tall, lean and stooped with a narrow wedge of a face, rusty side whiskers and a bare chin. He wore a suit of shiny blue serge and a bowler flat on top and turning green.

That was my first sight of Dugald McAlister and afterwards I never once saw him take the hat off his head.

"Electreecity," he was saying, "I learned thirty year ago in Aberdeen. That's in Scotland, ye ken. And worked in Weenipeg. Very cold, Weenipeg. And now my own company in Vancouver. Very wet. Electreecity, mon it's grand. But ye maun hae the richt machinery, and it dinnae come cheap."

"You can supply it?" Uncle Percy asked.

"Aye, and the best, only the best. That's steam."

"We thought of gasoline or diesel," said Hogarth.

"Na, na, they break doon every time. 'Tis steam ye'll be wantin' and a sweet engine I have in Vancouver already. Secondhand, but rebuilt wi' my own hands. A wee darlin', and cheaper in the end."

"How much?" said Hogarth.

"Losh, that depends, Gie me twa days to figger a bid and ye'll no get better from any mon. Poles, wires and all, guaranteed by contract. I canna say fairer."

After a couple of days the Directors seemed to be satisfied with McAlister's bid. I saw him and Hogarth sign some papers on

Uncle Percy's desk and took them for the contract. But I didn't know how much money would be spent. Plenty, I guessed.

When McAlister had left the office Foster said he doubted the electric machine could start up before Borden came to town.

"Not a chance," said Hogarth. "That Scotchman won't break a contract and pay us damages."

"We'd look pretty foolish if he did," Uncle Percy muttered.

"What would Borden think?"

"And the shareholders," said Brindle. "That's the main thing. We'll need a hell of a lot more money yet."

McAlister settled down in the Majestic after Miss Stella gave him a special rate and he worked fast.

The first cedar poles were soon brought from the North Thompson woods on flat cars and a gang of men from Vancouver began to set them up along the main streets. Another crew climbed them and strung the wires, half the town watching.

McAlister watched, too. He shouted at the men on the poles, made notes on slips of paper and mumbled to himself. Sometimes, in the evening, I'd see him through the window of the Majestic standing alone at the bar with two glasses in front of him, one for whisky, neat, and a large one for beer. He drank from them by turns but never spoke to his workmen at the other end of the bar. So long as he was in the room they didn't talk much, either.

In the kitchen Miss Stella told me that McAlister was a queer old cuss.

"Scotchmen, they're all like that," she said. "Mean and grouchy. But he knows his business."

The Corporation had bought the empty store down the street from the Majestic for the power house. McAlister's crew tore up the floor and laid a slab of concrete and built a brick chimney through the roof.

Before the job was finished he went to Vancouver to get the electric machinery. A week later the train brought it to town, packed in dozens of wooden crates. McAlister fussed and grumbled over his men as they unloaded the crates onto a wagon from the livery stable.

"Steady, lads," he kept saying. "They're easy broke, mind. Dinna hurry."

Tex and his Clydesdales took all day, with many trips back and forth, to haul the machinery to the power house. There I noticed a lanky, leathery young fellow with a drawling way of talk. McAlister had hired him in Vancouver to manage the plant. His name, I found out, was Gerry Todd.

"An American," Uncle Percy told me, "but he understands electricity. The Americans are often quite clever at that sort of thing."

When the last of the machinery was in the power house, just before dark, McAlister locked the door. He and Todd were back next morning and on the way to school I saw them opening the crates.

By afternoon, when I looked in again, bits and pieces of the steam engine lay scattered all over the cement floor.

They worked for the next month and gradually put the machinery together. The steam engine stood beside the chimney bolted into the cement slab under a flat boiler. A big flywheel was connected with a smaller wheel on the generator by a long belt and there were all kinds of other wheels and dials and levers. Wires and light bulbs dangled from the ceiling. The whole thing seemed to be in such a mess that I couldn't see how it would ever make electricity.

But in Uncle Percy's office, near the end of May, I heard McAlister tell the Directors that he'd be making a test in a day or two.

"Dinna fash yersels," he said. "Gie me the money owed and she'll be ready."

"That's not in the contract," said Hogarth. "You get paid off when the job's finished."

"Aye, the contract. But the extras, ye ken. Terrible, terrible. Na, na, it's the money I need to pay the wages and all."

"We'll think about it and let you know," said Hogarth.

McAlister went away, mumbling to himself.

The Corporation must have been running short of money

because Hogarth and Uncle Percy called at the Bank of Montreal next day and, I guessed, were raising a loan.

The machinery was to be tested two days before Borden arrived. All the windows of the power house had been covered with black cloth and only the Directors were allowed inside. But Uncle Percy took me along. It was part of my education, he said, and McAlister agreed if I kept my mouth shut. I promised.

He was in his shirt sleeves and bowler hat, Todd in overalls, both of them smeared with oil and, I thought, pretty nervous. A coal fire was roaring in the furnace, steam leaked out of the boiler pipes and the room was stifling hot. I wondered if the bulbs that dangled from the ceiling would really light up. The Directors had their eyes fixed on the bulbs, too.

"Mind, she may need a bit more work yet," said McAlister. "That's the way o' it wi electreecity. Now then, Todd, let her go!"

Todd jerked a lever, the big flywheel began to spin, the long belt tightened, the generator whirled and hummed, the bulbs flickered and suddenly the room was ablaze with light.

"By God, it works!" Hogarth yelled above the clank of the machinery.

"Aye, she'll do," McAlister yelled back. "Steam, ye canna beat it."

After a while Todd pulled the lever again. The engine stopped and the lights flickered out.

Uncle Percy shook McAlister's greasy hand.

"Amazing! Congratulations."

"Very good," said McAlister. "But the money, the extras. 'Tis all in the contract."

"No, no. Three months from the completion of the work the costs are to be reviewed. That's the contract."

"Three month!" cried McAlister. "And wi' bills and wages to pay! I'll be ruined."

Uncle Percy glanced at Hogarth. "Perhaps we could stretch a point?"

"But not till after a full test," said Hogarth. "Wait for Borden.

102

Then we'll see."

"Tisna honest. Tisna just," McAlister grumbled. "I'll hae the law on ye."

He was still whining and grumbling when the Directors left him with Todd in the power house and walked over to Uncle Percy's office. I tidied up the back room, pretending not to listen to their talk.

"He's a tough nut," said Brindle. "Think he'll go to court?"

"No chance," said Hogarth. "He's bluffin', that's all."

"Of course," Uncle Percy agreed. "But we've no time to waste. Borden's due the day after tomorrow and there's a lot to be done yet."

"And the bills," Hogarth growled. "We've run it too close. That note at the bank."

Foster scratched his little goat beard. "I'm worried, boys, I'm worried."

There must have been plenty for them to worry about.

The hall above the Central Emporium had been draped in red, white and blue bunting, with the huge Union Jack on the wall, the same as when McBride came to town. Electric bulbs, dozens of them, hung from the ceiling. On the raised guest table McAlister's crew had installed a wire and fixed a silver button to a polished block of mahogany wood. When Borden pushed the button, at exactly nine o'clock, the hall, the streets and stores would light up.

Uncle Percy was to be chairman of the banquet since Hogarth, the President of the Corporation, said he'd never made a speech in his life and didn't intend to start now.

Miss Stella and Lee Gung, her cook, were to provide the grub and her three housemaids would serve it with the help of some of us kids from school. The Fireman's Brass Band was rehearsing three nights a week to get "The Maple Leaf Forever" and "Rule Britannia" and "Hearts of Oak" down pat.

All the Corporation shareholders, about fifty of them, had been invited to the banquet and the *Echo* announced that "this historic occasion will be strictly non-political."

A cloth banner strung above the railway station hardly looked non-political to me. In letters a foot high it said "Emerald Vale Welcomes Robert Borden, Defender of Canada. No Reciprocity!"

The few Liberal shareholders didn't like that banner much but, as Uncle Percy told them, the Conservatives had given Laurier a warm welcome.

"Fair's fair," he said and the Liberals stopped arguing. They knew Borden couldn't win the election anyhow.

By this time the town seemed to have forgotten Reciprocity and talked about the wonder of automatic light. Even Jessup had begun to take it seriously. He described its history in the *Echo*, filling a solid page but, reading it, nobody could be sure whether Franklin, Edison or Borden had invented electricity.

On the afternoon of the great day, long before the special train was due, a noisy, happy crowd jammed the railway platform. Fire Chief Ben Stott, his black beard neatly trimmed, had drawn up the band in their scarlet uniforms at one end of the platform. The Directors stood at the other, with me huddling, unnoticed, behind them. Buggies, saddle horses and the Reo, borrowed from Miss Stella, were all mixed up together in the street. Borden's welcome, I guessed, would be even warmer than Laurier's.

At six o'clock, right on time, the train pulled in. The band struck up "The Maple Leaf Forever" but I could barely hear it through the scream of the engine's whistle, the clanging bell and the cheers of the crowd.

Borden was the first man to step down from the private car. I recognized him from his pictures in the papers, the ruff of gray hair parted in the middle, the rugged face and clipped mustache.

Uncle Percy shook his hand and introduced him to the Directors but his words were lost in the din.

The man following Borden from the car was the fattest I'd ever seen. A red mustache overspread the bloated cheeks and the wattles of his neck seemed likely to split the starched white collar.

"Who's that?" Foster shouted into Brindle's ear.

"That's Pinkham," Brindle shouted back.

I'd often heard of Oliver F. Pinkham, the Grit Cabinet Minister who'd broken with Laurier because he disagreed with Reciprocity. The *Echo* always called him Oily Oliver till he joined Borden but now he was mentioned in the editorials as "a giant of politics" or "a patriot who puts his country ahead of his party."

"So that's Pinkham," said Foster, "By God, I wouldn't trust him. The Grits never change."

While Uncle Percy finished the introductions Pinkham whispered to Borden out of the side of his mouth. Borden kept smiling but he didn't look as if he was enjoying the welcome, or Pinkham either.

The Band had got through "The Maple Leaf Forever" and started on "Rule Britannia," Chief Stott waving his baton and sweating hard.

At last the visitors were led to the Reo with Hogarth and Borden in the front seat, Uncle Percy and Pinkham in the rear. The band marched behind, now on "Hearts of Oak," but all I could hear was the beat of the drums and the roar of the people along the street. Then came the buggies and some cowboys on their cayuses. I drove our dog-cart, Brindle and Foster squeezed into the seat beside me.

"This beats Laurier all hollow," said Brindle.

It was seven o'clock, only two hours before the lights would be turned on, when Uncle Percy seated Borden on his right, Pinkham at his left at the head table, Hogarth, Brindle and Foster next to them. The shareholders of the Corporation filled the other tables and the waitresses from the Majestic hustled about to serve the dinner. The kids from school helped them, getting in each other's way and spilling a lot of food with a clatter of trays and dishes. My job was to look after the head table, running in and out of the kitchen.

Borden had stopped smiling and ate and drank little. Pinkham wolfed his meal, muttering under his huge mustache to Uncle Percy. As I filled and refilled his wine glass I could hear snatches of his talk and the word Reciprocity over and over again. Uncle Percy listened but kept looking at his watch and the electric button in front of Borden.

It was starting to get dark, around half past eight before Uncle Percy rose to make the welcoming speech.

"Mr. Borden, Mr. Pinkham and gentlemen," he said, "this being a strictly non-political occasion, a gathering of friends, I shall say only that our distinguished guest of honor, soon to be Prime Minister, stands four square, as did his immortal predecessor, John A. Macdonald, against the old conspiracy nowadays known as Reciprocity..."

"Annexation!" Pinkham snorted.

"...and I need not assure you that the Dominion of Canada will not submit..."

"For a mess of Yankee pottage."

"...to the betrayal of its future and..."

"Manifest Destiny! Never!"

"...the Empire of which it is a vital link in a golden chain encircling the world."

"Not with Laurier's tin-pot navy."

"And now," said Uncle Percy, "our guest may care to say a few words before he inaugurates the electrical age on this ever memorable night in our history."

The twilight had deepened and the room was almost dark as Borden got to his feet and the shareholders cheered and clapped their hands and waved their napkins.

I couldn't listen to his speech because all us kids had to carry the trays and dishes down the stairs and over to the Majestic.

When I returned to the hall it was a couple of minutes after nine. Uncle Percy stared at his watch and the electric button on the table.

"...your fine young city," Borden was saying, in his brisk, barking voice, "faces a prosperous future but the nation is in a grave crisis which involves its very existence. I am certain that the loyal citizens of Emerald Vale will respond to the challenge of Reciprocity and alien forces sinister and malevolent."

106

"Hear! Hear!" Pinkham growled. "Veiled treason!"

I could see that Uncle Percy was getting desperate. Suddenly he yanked his watch from his vest pocket and held it in front of Borden.

"Remember, my friends," Borden went on, "that your vote is needed to repel..."

He glanced down at the watch and paused.

"Ah yes," he said, "I now have the honor and the sincere pleasure to...to bring a new light, as it were, to the thriving community of...of Emerald Dale."

In the dead silence of the hall he leaned forward and pressed the button.

Nothing happened. I looked up at the electric bulbs but could hardly see them in the darkness. A murmur came from the crowd, a gasp from Brindle and a squeak from Foster.

"That goddamn Scotchman!" cried Hogarth.

Borden pressed the button again and again nothing happened.

Uncle Percy leaped from his chair and pounded the button with his fist. But the room was still dark.

In this crisis it was good to see how he kept his head.

"A misunderstanding, no doubt," he said. "If Mr. Borden will excuse me for a moment perhaps Mr. Pinkham would be kind enough to address you while I..."

He didn't finish the sentence but turned and dashed out the back door and down the stairs with me at his heels. I followed him across the street to the power house.

McAlister was standing in the doorway. Behind him I heard the whir of machinery and the electric bulbs blazed above it. But the wires to the banquet hall and the town must have been switched off.

"What's this?" Uncle Percy shouted.

McAlister thrust out his naked chin. "The contract, ye ken. Aye, the extras."

"The extras? They'll be reviewed in three months. That's the contract."

"I canna wait three month. There's bills to pay."

"Outrageous! We'll sue you! The Corporation..."

McAlister jabbed a greasy finger into Uncle Percy's shirt front and left a smear on it.

"Och, the Corporation! Ye think I dinna ken the Corporation's broke? Nae money, nae electreecity. That's the way o' it."

Uncle Percy stepped back and glared at McAlister as if the man were crazy.

"Very well then," he said. "I'll give you a cheque."

"Nae cheques, mon. It's cash I'm wantin! A thousand dollar, and we'll talk about the rest tomorrow."

Uncle Percy's mouth fell open. "Cash? You expect me to have a thousand dollars in my pocket?"

"But ye'll know where to get it."

McAlister pointed at the Majestic on the corner. "Aye, she's got plenty, Miss Stella."

Uncle Percy glared at McAlister again, began to say something but closed his mouth and ran down the street. I watched him burst through the front door of the hotel and McAlister watched, too, with a crooked grin. Todd stood by the machinery, his hand on a big switch.

"Get ready," McAlister told him.

We waited for maybe five minutes and then Uncle Percy came running back. He was clutching a brown envelope and panting fit to burst.

"Here it is," he gasped. "But you'll pay for this, by God, you'll pay dear in court."

"Dinna fash yersel', mon," said McAlister.

He took the envelope from Uncle Percy's hand and tore it open and riffled through the green bills, his lips moving as he counted them.

"Verra guid," he muttered. "But only on account, mind. Ye'll get it, the electreecity. All right, Todd."

"You swine!" Uncle Percy shouted but didn't even wait for a receipt. He ran to the Emporium, his coat tails flying, and I followed him up the stairs.

The hall was nearly pitch dark but Pinkham seemed to be in the middle of a speech, his voice hoarse, his wattles swelling.

"Reciprocity!" I heard him bawl. "The ultimate betrayal, the crime against..."

Uncle Percy squeezed past him to the table.

"Excuse me," he panted and pushed the button.

All the electric bulbs blazed out. Everybody jumped up and cheered, everybody but Borden. He sat there chewing his mustache and I thought he was trying to hide a smile. Pinkham kept talking but nobody listened. At the far end of the hall Jessup and the reporters from Vancouver were scribbling in their notebooks.

When the train pulled out just before midnight Uncle Percy drove Brindle and me back to town in the dog cart.

"It went pretty well," said Brindle. "Thanks to Stella. But that Scotch bastard!"

"Indeed," Uncle Percy muttered.

"And Borden's a pretty good talker, but not as good as Laurier and that's a fact."

"Perhaps. Does it matter?"

"It will in the election, you can bet. I don't like the smell of things."

"No fear," said Uncle Percy. "The country won't vote for Reciprocity and Laurier's tin-pot navy'll sink him anyway."

As we drove past the power house McAlister was standing at the doorway again, silhouetted against the lights inside.

Uncle Percy reined in the colt and scowled down at the tall, stooped figure in the flat bowler.

"So you got your pound of flesh, Mr. McAlister. But you'll pay for it. And damages too, high damages."

McAlister pointed a greasy finger to the lights flaming on the big sign above the Majestic.

"Na, na, ye got a bargain. There's electreecity, and cheap, ye ken, at any price. Mon, it's grrand."

Men of Genius

The only two men of genius in Emerald Vale were discovered by my Uncle George, Aunt Minerva's younger brother from New York. He said he would immortalize them and I guess he did. Probably no one else could have done it because Uncle George was a kind of genius himself.

As he stepped off the train he seemed a very ordinary little man except for his clothes. His suit was cut in the latest American style, pinched at the waist but flaring out over the peg-top pants. His boots were made of well-shined patent leather and gray cloth uppers with pearl buttons.

Uncle George was short, about the same height as Aunt Minerva, but he didn't look at all like his chubby sister. His face was thin and pale as if he'd lived indoors too much, his nose long and hooked, his silky black mustache no thicker than his eyebrows.

Uncle Percy warned me in advance that Uncle George was no ordinary man. He'd graduated from Harvard and made a lot of money all over the States in banking, publishing, real estate and I don't know what else. But somehow he'd lost several fortunes through no fault of his own. Now, I gathered, he was taking a holiday while he planned some important new enterprise.

"He's gone through four marriages already," Uncle Percy said, "and taken out his American papers. But never mention it in front of your aunt. Remember, he's family."

Uncle George began to make his discovery of genius as soon as he arrived in town. We were sitting on the verandah sipping lemonade and slapping mosquitoes, too hot for talk in the muggy twilight. I'd just heard the first rumble of thunder and seen a faint flash of lightning over the Porcupine Range when Uncle George squirmed in his rattan chair and picked up a pamphlet from the table beside him.

"What's this?" he grunted and held the pamphlet up to the electric light.

I knew what it was, of course. All the kids in school had read the pamphlet and bought extra copies for ten cents apiece as the best joke since the Riel movie.

A thousand copies had been printed on the *Echo*'s job press and all were sold in a week. The flimsy green cover introduced "Emeralds from the Vale, by Hank Dutton, the Cowboy Lariat." Under the type was a crude drawing of a lariat hanging from the horn of a stock saddle.

Uncle George burst out laughing. "The Poet Lariat! A brilliant pun. My, my, that's wit. And who's Hank Dutton?"

"A ranch hand, a cowpuncher," said Uncle Percy. "He used to be a rodeo rider and a champion, too, I believe, till he lost an arm in some accident and started to write doggerel, ghastly stuff, unbelievable, but Hank's quite harmless and everybody's sorry for the poor chap."

"He punches cows with one arm?"

"Actually he's a kind of janitor, waits on table and helps the cook at the Hogarth ranch. Hogarth took pity on him."

Uncle George glanced at the second page of the pamphlet and chuckled again. "Listen to this..."

"Oh, spare us," said Aunt Minerva.

"No, no, it's too good to miss—"Ode to Electricity," if you please, rich, gorgeous poesy, unpremeditated song."

Aunt Minerva couldn't stop him and he read the opening poem aloud, intoning it like an actor. But I'd read it so often that it didn't seem funny to me any more.

> The scientific miracle of electricity
> Has brought us all a new felicity
> And also strengthened the bonds of domesticity.
> The houses are now full of light
> And the streets bright even at midnight
> Thanks to the Emerald Vale Power Corporation
> Which deserves our warm approbation.

"Stop, George, stop!" cried Aunt Minerva.

"Absurd," said Aunt Lizzy, her glass beads tinkling. "Vulgar, disgusting."

Uncle George smiled down at his two sisters and flashed his big white teeth with their gold fillings. "Here's another gem from the Vale..."

"I can't stand it!" Aunt Minerva cried again but Uncle George read out the "Ode to Canada."

> The early days of Canada are hidden in mystery
> But afterwards it had a thrilling history.
> The Indians fought with tortures and crimes
> But the white men beat them back many times.
> The nation was saved by the brave General Brock
> Who laid down his life on Queenston Rock.
> Then Macdonald built our glorious Dominion
> Without equal anywhere in my humble opinion.
> Now Laurier would destroy it by his mad Reciprocity
> But Canadians won't stand for such an atrocity.
> Britannia rules the waves, the Maple Leaf Forever,
> The Conservative party saves us, the Liberal Party never.

"Oh, loving God," Uncle Percy murmured.

Uncle George wouldn't stop. "Here's a biblical theme—they found the infant Moses in the river amid bullrushes and willows and he had no blankets or pillows..."

"Shush!" Aunt Minerva groaned.

Uncle George had started to pace back and forth across the verandah.

"You don't understand," he said. "There's good poetry and bad poetry and if it's bad enough it's good. But it has to be really bad. Then it's a collector's item, priceless. Yes, and your Hank Dutton qualifies—the genuine article, a bad poet, a natural genius."

"You're talking rubbish," said Aunt Minerva.

Uncle George waved the green pamphlet in her face.

"Ever hear of the great William McGonagall? No? At Harvard we took a course in bad poems, literary curiosa, wonderful fun, comic relief. McGonagall was our idol, the worst poet in the English language. They cheered him and they jeered him but his stuff sold like hot cakes. He took it all in deadly earnest, called himself a poet and tragedian and made a pile. Why, I can remember even now..."

"No more, no more," Aunt Minerva gasped.

"Wait," said Uncle George. "Yes, I've got it, word for word, McGonagall's immortal tribute to General Gordon, the martyr of Khartoum. Bad poets seem to have an affinity for generals—Gordon in England, Brock in Canada. Listen..."

Still pacing the verandah, he flung out his arms and recited the immortal tribute.

> I hope the people will his memory revere
> And take an example from him and worship God in fear,
> And never be too fond of worldly gear,
> And walk in General Gordon's footsteps while they are here.

Uncle George beamed at his sister. "That's what I call genius. And Hank's as bad as McGonagall, even worse. There's money in it, I tell you."

"Fiddlesticks," said Aunt Minerva.

114

"You think so, eh? Well, I was in the book business long enough to know what sells. All Hank needs is a little promotion. Yes, yes, I must see this native prodigy."

"I wouldn't," said Uncle Percy. "He'll fix you with his glittering eye and bore you numb with more doggerel. Sometimes he even talks in rhyme. It is automatic, a disease almost like Saint Vitus' Dance. Poor Hank."

"Aha, this gets better and better."

"But his prose is the worst of it," Uncle Percy went on. "He bought a dictionary and I lent him some books when he was in hospital—a fatal mistake. Now he comes out with the damndest gibberish, big words he doesn't understand. Extraordinary."

"Trippingly off the tongue," said Uncle George. "Just lead me to the genius."

Next morning I harnessed the colt to the dog-cart and drove Uncle George out to Hogarth's spread. We found Hank on the corral fence watching a couple of cowboys branding and castrating some Hereford calves. I'd seen the job so often that it didn't interest me and I'd given up the idea of being a cowboy myself. Now I planned to be a doctor or locomotive engineer or something high class like that.

Uncle George took one look at the squealing calves on the ground and turned away. "Horrible," he grunted.

Hank caught sight of us and raised his left hand, his only one. The right sleeve of his red shirt was pinned to his chest.

"Howdy, folks," he said. "A lovely day."

When he frowned and glanced up at the sky for a moment I knew what was coming. It always did.

"After the thunder the morning's a wonder, dew on the sage, the earth opens a new page. Howdy!"

"I wouldn't have believed it," Uncle George whispered to me. "Poet Lariat to the life, by God!"

Hank climbed down from the fence and stretched out his single hand. He was a tall man, a foot higher than Uncle George, and about thirty years old, I guessed, with a face tanned and drawn tight like rawhide and stiff ginger-colored hair. He usually wore a sly grin and had a way of winking a steel-blue eye as if to share some private joke.

I introduced him to my Uncle George from New York.

"Never bin in New York," said Hank, "but mighty proud to meet you, George. Put it there."

I saw Uncle George wince under the grip of Hank's brown fingers but he managed to say it was a pleasure.

"Likewise," Hank grinned. "But it's gettin' hot. Let's set a while on the porch. Cooler in the shade."

We followed him to the log bunkhouse and sat on the porch while Hank rolled a cigarette with his one hand, licked it and struck a match on his patched cowboy boot.

"I've read your book," Uncle George began. "Admirable, excellent."

"That there was no book," said Hank. "Jest a little experiment to see how she'd go."

"It went well, very well. And you must have more poems."

"Scads of 'em. Like the fella says, the best is yet to come."

Again the shy grin. "It's a gift, I reckon."

"A gift," Uncle George agreed. "A rare gift."

"But you got to work at it. Yeah, it comes and goes—the inspiration, the afflatus, like the fella says, the muse."

"The muse of course. Very rare. Read much poetry, Hank?"

"Quite a bit. Percy lent me some books, good ones, too. But I don't aim to imitate nobody. Keep it original, eh?"

"You're right. Keep it original."

"Yeah, I even read some Shakespeare stuff. He was an English fella and smart. It sounds pretty good but don't rhyme up. Then I seen I was writin' the same as him and mine was good, too, but it wasn't me, y'understand. Not me. So I left him alone."

Hank looked up at the sky and another frown puckered his forehead. I knew he was searching for some big, fancy words.

"The way it is," he said, "I'm under the jurisdiction of inscrutable destiny."

116

Uncle George pulled a handkerchief from his pocket to blow his nose.

"Inscrutable, yes," he muttered. "But I see you write in the classic vein, heroic couplets, Pope's style, iambic pentameter."

"Yeah, iambic pentameter, that's my favorite. But not Pope. I'm no Catholic, y'understand. Raised a Methodist, strict, mighty strict at home. But you know how it is, eh? Like the fella says, the world's too much with us."

"Ah, Wordsworth. The Romantic Revival."

"Oh sure, I'm romantic. Nothin' wrong with romance."

Again the frown. Then, "Take your romance at every chance. Follow your own star, no matter how far. That's Emerson."

Now the shy grin. "It gets to be a habit."

"No need to apologize, Hank," said Uncle George. "Follow your star."

"I aim to, yeah."

"But there's one theme missing from your poetry—a love interest."

"You mean dirty stuff? No, sir, I never write dirty."

"Of course not. I mean clean love, romantic love, innocent. The public expects it from a major poet."

Hank's face turned red under the tan.

"Well, I started a little poem about that Egypt lady at the theatre in Kamloops last week, the belly dancer."

"What! A belly dancer?"

"Yeah, but clean, absolutely clean, y'understand. Every part of her a-shakin' not jest her belly. From head to toe, up and down and sideways. I never seen the like of it—beautiful."

"Ah, the poetry of motion!"

"That's it!" cried Hank. "You got it. The poetry of motion."

"And a beautiful face, too, I dare say," Uncle George suggested.

"Oh, the face. Well, sir, I didn't notice the face particular. I wasn't aimin' to be technical."

Uncle George had to blow his nose again.

"You wrote a poem about her?" he asked.

"Jest a little stanza or so, nothin' much."

"All the same I'd like to see it."

Hank went into the bunkhouse and came back with a kid's scribbler like the ones we used in school. Thumbing through the pages, he found the stanza on the Egypt lady and read it aloud in a funny sing-song voice.

> Ancient Egypt invented the art of belly dancing
> And even in Kamloops today it is still entrancing.
> The dancer shakes all of her, not merely the belly
> Every limb quakes like a saucer of jelly.
> A vision of beauty, electric, ethereal,
> Reaching towards Heaven and regions sidereal,
> Searching the sky for the universal whole,
> Done right, the dance is a mirror of the human soul.

Hank closed the scribbler, his cheeks burning. "It's not right yet. I'll polish it up one of these days."

"You must, Hank, you must," said Uncle George. "But surely you saw the lady outside the theatre, met her personally?"

"No, I couldn't. I'd of bought her dinner or somethin' but"—he paused, seeking the right word—"I was in the fell grip of circumstances like the fella says. Dead broke—a little poker game y'understand. So I come home."

Hank looked at the Porcupine Range for a long moment. Then he added: "Her name was Fatima on the billboard. But she wasn't fat. No, sir, shaped perfect, legs like a thoroughbred. And her real name, I found out, was Susan—Susan Elwell, a pretty name, eh? She come from a farm near Lethbridge, learned dancin' somewheres in the States. I'll never see her again, godammit."

"But she'll inspire even better work," said Uncle George. "And in the meantime, Hank, I've got a proposition for you. How about a swell book, all your poems printed in style on the best paper? We split even, fifty-fifty. How about it?"

"Hell, who'd print it? Who'd buy it?"

"Leave that to me," Uncle George told him. "We could make a

pile of money together. And perhaps stage appearances as well, reading your poetry, in vaudeville like Fatima. Why, you might meet her somewhere on the circuit."

"Now you're talkin' George! Yeah, vodeville. I'd like that fine."

Uncle George had another idea. "Can you still swing a lariat, Hank, with your—ugh—amputation? It'd help, add verisimilitude, a nice cowboy touch—the Poet Lariat in person."

"I sure can," said Hank.

He took a braided cowhide lariat from a peg, spread a loop above his head, twirled it around his boots and jumped in and out of it, nimble as a boy.

Uncle George's mouth opened wide. "Superb! The poet and the lariat. Just exactly right for the stage."

"Not like the Egypt lady," said Hank, "but maybe it'll do."

After some more talk there on the porch the deal was made, without a written word, only a handshake.

"Between gentlemen," Uncle George explained. But I thought the whole thing was crazy.

We drove away and Uncle George brought the scribbler with him. He kept chuckling as he glanced through it.

"Even beats McGonagall. Hank's under the jurisdiction of inscrutable destiny—refuses to write like Shakespeare—and the Egypt lady quaking and shaking, ethereal, sidereal but absolutely clean! That's genius, by God, sheer genius. Yes, yes, there's money in it."

When we reached town Uncle George caught sight of the paintings in the window of the bake shop along with the pies and tarts.

"Stop," he said, and got out of the cart to peer through the window. I thought he was going to buy some of the butter tarts that Aunt Minerva sometimes gave us for dessert, a special treat, expensive at 20 cents a dozen. But he was looking at the pictures.

"Who did them?" he asked me.

I pointed to the sign above the front door—Fritz Heinrich, Home Made Baker.

"What! The baker is a painter?"

119

"He thinks he is," I said.

"Well, he is, too. An original, primitive but original. A second genius in a one-horse town. Amazing."

Uncle George looked up at the sign again. "The Home Made Baker. With a touch of Brueghel."

I'd never heard of Brueghel and didn't know what Uncle George was driving at. But I guessed he had another of his crazy ideas from Harvard.

All I knew was that Fritz was the only baker in town and a good one. Even Aunt Minerva said so, and Marie was jealous of him because she couldn't make butter tarts like his.

Fritz lived alone in a room above the shop. When he wasn't baking he painted those weird pictures on cardboard or rolls of wallpaper and tried to sell them. Nobody except Miss Stella ever bought any. She had three, a yard square, hung behind the bar in the Majestic. They were full of horses and cows and barns and mountains and funny-looking people, all painted worse than a kid could do them in school.

Miss Stella must have been sorry for Fritz. She took most of his bread and cakes for the hotel dining room. But everybody else laughed at Fritz's paintings. Until the cowhands got tired of talking about them they used to say that the fetlocks of his horses were too long, the withers too high and the hocks out of joint. So they were but Fritz would never make them right.

"I vant to baint," he would tell me when I sometimes watched him working back of the shop. "Und I baint like I see." He also wanted to go to an art school in New York or Paris and learn to paint better but he couldn't raise the money. Like Miss Stella, I felt kind of sorry for Fritz, even if he was a German and didn't understand horses.

Uncle George kept peering through the window and muttering to himself. Now he asked me to wait and went into the shop. It was empty but he opened the door behind it and found Fritz in the bake room, sitting on a stool and kneading dough in a big wooden tub with his bare feet.

120

Fritz reminded me of the horses in the paintings, his legs too long, his arms too thin, his hands too big. His bony face was always smeared white with flour, his dangling hair the color of his butter tarts. Poor Fritz, I thought, he's getting old, almost forty, and he'll never learn to paint.

Through the back window I saw Uncle George talking to him but couldn't hear what they said. Fritz stopped kneading the dough and wiped his feet with a towel and took some pictures from a cupboard. Uncle George held them up to the light, still talking, and Fritz seemed to be pleased. A smile broke through the flour on his cheeks as Uncle George studied the pictures.

They talked for quite a while till I was getting hungry and the colt restless. At last Uncle George came out of the shop, a bundle of pictures rolled under his arm, and got into the dog cart.

"What a morning!" he chortled. "Two geniuses, the poet and the painter. Both bad enough to be good. Yes sir, and there's money in it."

When we were home he told Uncle Percy and Aunt Minerva that he had a double deal.

"All fair and square. Plenty for Hank and Fritz and only the usual commission for me."

Aunt Minerva snorted.

"Who'd ever buy those dreadful poems?"

"Or those impossible daubs?" Uncle Percy muttered.

"You'd be surprised," said Uncle George. "Primitive art, unfettered by convention, stream of consciousness, all that—it's the rage down east. Just snobbery, of course, piffle, but it sells like hot cakes if you know the market."

"Poppycock!" cried Aunt Minerva. "You and your market. Come off it, George."

"I shouldn't like to see those chaps disappointed," said Uncle Percy. "A shame to raise their hopes and then..."

"No, no," Uncle George declared. "They'll make plenty, never fear. This is strictly business, and I know business."

"You ought to by now," said Aunt Minerva.

"Indeed," Uncle Percy murmured under his breath.

They argued back and forth all through lunch and Uncle George seemed to win in the end. With a temporary loan from Aunt Minerva out of her housekeeping money he left on the night train for Vancouver, taking Hank's scribbler and Fritz's pictures in his valise.

When we were alone together Uncle Percy warned me not to talk about Aunt Minerva's brother.

"It'd only worry her," he said. "A family matter—you understand?"

I understood all right and didn't talk about it at school.

We heard nothing from Uncle George for a couple of months and I guessed the double deal had fallen through. Hank heard nothing, either, but he kept writing in his scribblers. The next time I rode out to the Hogarth spread he told me he was expanding his poem on the belly dancer to more than a hundred lines and called it "a lyric idyll." Hank must have been gutting the dictionary.

One Saturday night he was in town and the cowboys were drinking in the bunk house. Somebody got hold of the lyric idyll and started to read it aloud everybody laughing fit to be tied. Then Hank came home and knocked him down, leaving his nose bloody and crooked. Hank had only one arm but it was mighty strong. After that he kept the scribblers padlocked in a chest under his bunk.

But I saw from his looks that he was worrying about Uncle George. So was Fritz, who turned out more pictures than bread. I could hardly get a word from him when I was sent to his shop for butter tarts.

"That other Uncle of yours," Miss Stella told me as I was eating pie in the Majestic kitchen, "he's a crook. Not like Percy. A cheap con man. Poor Minerva."

For once Miss Stella was wrong.

Early in September Hank and Fritz got letters from Uncle George. He'd sold the copyright on Hank's poems to a New York publisher and a store in Chicago wanted all the pictures Fritz could

122

paint. Uncle George asked them both to meet him in Seattle right away and arrange for "promotion and personal appearances, all expenses paid."

"Well I never!" said Aunt Minerva, "Ha! That George and his market. But I don't like the smell of it."

"And those Americans," Uncle Percy grumbled. "Extraordinary people, extraordinary."

I guess they were, too, but that didn't seem to matter.

Hank quit his job at the ranch, Fritz closed his bake shop and they went off on the same train, through Spokane to Seattle.

"They'll soon be back," Miss Stella told me.

She was wrong again.

Just before Christmas Uncle George sent Aunt Minerva a book in fancy leather binding, with gold letters on the cover, "Emeralds from the Vale, by Hank Dutton, the Cowboy Poet Lariat."

Aunt Minerva looked at it and began to giggle. "Oh, that George! I can't believe it."

But there it was, the book and Hank's photo inside. It showed him whirling a lariat and the old grin on his rawhide face.

Uncle George enclosed a cheque to repay Aunt Minerva's loan and a bunch of clippings from the American papers, with more photos of Hank on handbills from vaudeville theatres all over the States.

Most of the papers treated Hank as a big laugh and printed interviews to make him look silly. At some university in Ohio the students had given him a banquet and so far as I could make out it ended in a brawl. But everybody seemed to like Hank as they put him, pretty drunk I guessed, on the train. "The Poet Lariat," the Denver Post reported, "writes the worst poetry of the age since the work of the immortal Scotchman, McGonagall. And yet he is a character, another immortal in his fashion."

"Poor chap," said Uncle Percy, "they've ruined him."

Like Miss Stella, Uncle Percy was wrong. They hadn't ruined Hank.

At Christmas he wrote Uncle Percy and said he was doing fine and saving up his money to buy a little place on Fury Creek, next to the Hogarth spread. This was confidential but maybe Uncle Percy could get a price on the land without telling anyone.

"The papers down here," Hank added, "have a high old time kidding me along but I don't care, they're jealous, the joke is sure on them, and I get the money, you bet."

At the end of the letter there was a post script: "I met up with that little lady, you know who, and George is sweet on her but it won't work, him being so old. More anon."

Fritz seemed to be doing fine, too. He couldn't paint enough pictures to keep up with the demand for primitive art, George wrote from San Francisco. But he'd decided to take up another kind of painting at an art school in Chicago.

"It's a pity," said Uncle George. "He's infatuated with this new-fangled abstract stuff and it's unsaleable. I've told him but he won't listen. Alas, alas for the Home Made Baker. My own business plans will take me to Boston and, I believe, great opportunities. Hank has worn out the welcome of the American public, but he's stage-struck and I doubt you'll ever see him again in Emerald Vale."

Uncle George was wrong, too.

"They'll both be back," Miss Stella told me and this time she was right.

Fritz came first in the following summer. He had grown a shaggy beard, the color of his long hair and butter tarts, and he wore a white linen suit with peg-top pants and shiny patent leather shoes. All his primitive paintings had been sold but he refused to paint any more of them. His new abstract style wouldn't sell and no wonder. When he re-opened the bake shop and put a bunch of them in the window they looked like the smears and whirls of a blind man or a lunatic.

Fritz tried to explain them to me but his English hadn't improved and all I understood was that they were a kind of dream.

"It's de movement," he said. "Ja, de mind outside de body, it moves free—*Weltansicht*."

124

Fritz's mind may have moved free but he had to knead the dough again with his bare feet, because he'd spent all his money. That didn't leave much time for his art. Miss Stella bought three of his abstract pictures for the Majestic bar and hung them beside the old primitives. The cowboys soon got tired of laughing at them. But I thought Fritz seemed happy enough with his home-made bread, his dream and his *Weltansicht,* whatever that was.

Hank turned up next autumn in a brand new outfit of fringed buckskin and tooled leather boots that must have cost all of ten dollars. Nobody paid much heed to him on the station platform. Everybody looked at the wife clinging to his single arm. Fatima, or Susan Elwell, the Egypt lady from Lethbridge, was just as pretty as he'd claimed, like a china doll in her feathered hat and black fur coat that must have cost a hundred dollars—pretty but shy and blushing among strangers. She didn't look like a belly dancer to me.

The Hank Duttons seemed to adore each other. They settled down in their little spread beside Fury Creek and started to raise Shetland ponies for sale because Hank couldn't handle a beef herd with his one arm. But he could still write as well as ever and he wrote a lot more poetry.

When the city publishers were no longer interested he got out a new book for himself entitled *Rhymes from the Range and Elsewhere.* It was printed at Hank's expense on the *Echo's* new job press on the best paper with only a few mistakes in the type set by Alf Gropp.

Two special copies, for Susan and Uncle Percy, were covered in real leather and lettered in gold. On the first blank page of Uncle Percy's copy Hank wrote a lovely inscription.

> These poems are dedicated to my old friend Percy
> And judging them he will show his usual mercy.
> If I have been guilty of some foolish pranks
> He will forgive them and has my thanks.
> With gratitude in every clime and latitude
> Eternal friendship is my sincere attitude.

Uncle Percy was touched but couldn't bring himself to read the poems and put the book away on the shelf beside the *Encyclopedia Britannica*.

"Later perhaps," he muttered.

"Never, never," said Aunt Minerva.

At the livery stable Tex had somehow got hold of a copy and read it straight through.

"Hank's plum loco, always was," he told me. "But his gal, she'll do. Too bad we won't get to see that belly dance. She's too busy."

Mrs. Hank Dutton, as the whole town knew, was busy with the Shetland ponies and a baby expected before long and Hank was all of a twitter.

One spring evening, when I happened to ride past their place, I found him sitting on the corral fence and asked after Susan. He said she was near her time but doing fine.

"And to think," he added, "that old George was sweet on her! Yeah, he got a little fresh, in Detroit it was, and I hadda cool him down a little. But it didn't hurt much except for the black eye. There was nothin' personal in it, y'understand, and he took the hint and vamoosed out of town mighty quick."

I could see by his puckered forehead that Hank was going to break into automatic verse and he did. "That old demon lover soon took cover once I worked him over."

Then Hank ran out of rhymes and stared at Fury Creek.

"Great," I said, "but sounds like Coleridge. We read him in school."

"Yeah," Hank admitted, "but all us poets feed on each other."

The last we heard, Uncle George had married for the fifth time to some rich Boston heiress. "Wish me luck," he said in a letter to Aunt Minerva.

"Ha, he'll need it," she snorted.

"Indeed," said Uncle Percy.

Tex was right. None of us ever got to see the belly dance. But the Shetland ponies sold like hot cakes in Vancouver and the baby boy, when his mother brought him to our house, looked healthy

126

and the dead spit of Hank. Or so he wrote in his masterpiece, the Ode to Motherhood. I remember only its opening lines.

Every Canadian child has a human mother,
It must be her and no other.

We all thought Hank's third book was up to the standard of the first two but it didn't sell like hot cakes.

The Scientific Method

Paul Jessup, the *Echo*'s reporter, probably had more schooling than anyone in Emerald Vale but it didn't seem to do him much good. "If he ain't a horse's ass they don't make 'em no more," Tex used to say, and Uncle Percy called Jessup "a preposterous pedant" with dangerous political theories.

Why Mike Brindle kept him on the paper no one really knew, except that he worked hard and gathered a lot of news and never complained if his weekly pay cheque was late. But when Jessup discovered the Leporidae and the talking monkey and then got mixed up with General Custer and the massacre of the Little Big Horn that was more than even Brindle could stand. He fired Jessup for the last time.

Frank Halleck, the doctor's boy, started the trouble and I must have been a fool to help him. He wasn't my kind of a friend anyhow—too fat and clumsy to ride a horse or play baseball, his round face covered with pimples and he seldom stopped giggling. But I liked him, now and then, as a change from the other kids. They called him the Professor, or the Prof, because he read so many books and knew everything.

After he showed me a book of Indian history with pictures of fish and horses painted on rocks somewhere in the States one thing led to another. We found a chunk of granite just off the road between the Vale and the Quintlam Reserve and we drew some pictures on it with red paint like those in the book. When they were half dry we smeared them with dirt to make them look old.

A couple of days later we met Jessup coming out of the print shop and told him about the pictures. But we said they were a secret and not for publication in the *Echo*. Of course he pedaled his bicycle down the Quintlam road, taking along his box camera. The next issue of the paper ran two columns on "the art of the ancient Indian culture long undetected in this region."

Jessup even sold the story to the *Vancouver Gazette* and it published two of his snapshots. They were fuzzy but you could make out the fish and the horses. Brindle thought the *Echo* had a mighty big scoop till chief Barnabas came laughing into the shop and said it was all a fake.

"I seen that rock, huntin' last week," he told Brindle, "and there was no pitchers on it. Somebody's pullin' your leg, Mike. Kids, likely."

When Jessup got back to the shop Brindle fired him but he was at work again next morning as always happened.

We kept out of Jessup's way for a while. Then the Prof had a still better idea. He'd found the dry skeleton of some small animal near the school privy and took it home and read some medical books in his dad's office. "It's only a cat," he said, "but it might be anything. Jessup wouldn't know the difference if we fixed it up a bit."

So we fixed up the skull of the cat by yanking out the teeth and putting them back again upside down. Now they curved outwards and we'd never seen any animal with teeth like that.

"What's it supposed to be?" I asked the Prof.

He said the skull reminded him of a Procyon Lotor or maybe one of the Leporidea, a species spread all over the world, according to the books. They meant nothing to me but sounded fine.

We spent an hour, locked in my bedroom with Uncle Percy's Oxford dictionary, writing a long letter. The Prof typed it on his dad's typewriter in the evening when the office was empty, using the best paper he could find. It was a pretty good job, considering that he used only two fingers and made very few spelling mistakes.

It was tricky to choose the right signature but finally the Prof scrawled Whittier Franklin across the bottom of the letter. From what we'd read in our school history books those names seemed just right for a Yankee.

Franklin wrote that he was a doctor of science in Princeton University and had been studying the fauna of central British Columbia all summer. In the Monashee Range, east of Kamloops, he had made "a discovery certain to astound the science of biology, the skull of a quadruped mammal recently deceased, never before identified north of Mexico and supposedly extinct for at least five centuries. In my judgment it is of the species Leporidae or Felidae or possibly the Muridae as indicated by the reverse dental curvature unique to these arboreal carnivora."

Franklin couldn't be sure without further study and unfortunately he'd been called to his home in Princeton by illness in his family "but your reputation, Mr. Jessup, and your articles in the press, encourage my hope that you will complete the investigation of this specimen which I venture to send you herewith."

Nobody but the Prof, I thought, could have written that letter. We put it and the skull into a cardboard shoe box addressed to Jessup. The following week, when I went to Kamloops to have my teeth bands checked, I mailed the package there.

Jessup must have got it after a day or two but he said nothing to anyone. We saw him at the *Echo* with books spread over his desk, the skull nowhere in sight. It looked like our trick wasn't going to work.

"Don't worry," the Prof giggled, "he'll break out before long."

The Prof was right. While Brindle was away, visiting his sister in Vernon, Jessup broke out in the *Echo* with a front page headline:

WORLD OF SCIENCE ASTOUNDED BY LOCAL
DISCOVERY.

Dr. Franklin's letter and a long piece on the Leporidea and Muridae filled the whole front page. In a nice final touch Jessup wrote that "the Monashee Mystery revised all previous knowledge of these species."

The *Vancouver Gazette* picked up the story and ran it on the front page, too. Jessup had a query from Toronto and sent a telegraph dispatch to the *Globe*. Everybody in the Vale was talking about the Monashee Mystery.

"Oh boy, oh boy," the Prof snickered, "we've astounded the world of science good and plenty. Just wait."

We didn't have to wait long. In its next issue the *Echo* reported that the skull of the Monashee Mystery had been sent to the government museum in Victoria "for study and the results are anticipated with universal interest."

At the end of a week the results came in a short note from the curator of the museum. "The skull," he wrote, "is that of a Felis domestica or common domestic cat, the teeth misplaced, presumably by some mischievous person."

Brindle arrived home in time to read the note, his pasty face turning scarlet, his double chin shaking. He fired Jessup again and printed an editorial apologizing to the *Echo*'s readers for "a regrettable but innocent mistake." Jessup sulked three days before returning to work.

The Prof and I kept out of his way and couldn't tell if he suspected us. We didn't care much anyhow because everybody was talking about something else by now. For the first time a circus came to town that autumn.

It was a second-class circus, Uncle Percy said, with only one ring. But it looked mighty grand to me when they unloaded the animals from two special railway cars, a lion and a brown Russian bear in cages and a real elephant, the only one I'd ever seen, with huge flapping ears and a long trunk curling and uncurling.

The parade down the main street was led by a man in a top hat and red tail-coat riding a milk white horse. The cages on wheels were pulled by more white horses and some good-looking ladies rode in open carriages with fancy gold trimmings. They smiled and waved to the crowd.

The last rig was different from the others, a little green cart like a toy pulled by a donkey. The man in the seat had bristling whiskers, a green uniform and a tall peaked hat. He never smiled or waved but stared straight ahead as if he hated the town and the show. A sign hanging from the cart said he was "Herr Julius Finklemann and Otto, the World's Only Talking Monkey."

At first I didn't see any monkey. Then a tiny animal sprang up to the man's shoulder. It was dressed in a green uniform like his and their hairy faces looked almost the same, too. They might have been father and son. The monkey seemed to be chattering but I couldn't hear him in all the noise.

As the parade went slowly through the town the Prof and I ran behind it to the rodeo grounds. There we watched a gang of roustabouts drive in wooden pegs and before noon a canvas tent rose like a big toadstool. The cages, the fancy rigs and the toy cart were scattered around it in a circle. The elephant, chained to a post, was lifting swatches of hay to his mouth with his trunk. But we didn't see Finklemann and his monkey or any of the circus folks and guessed they were inside the tent.

"You think it can really talk?" The Prof asked me.

Jessup was standing beside us with his note book and box camera. "Of course not," he said. "No monkey can talk. Impossible. Not even the higher anthropoids."

The Prof began to giggle. "Maybe he's another extinct species and he'll astound the world of science."

Jessup glared at him through his thick glasses and walked off, muttering.

"There goes the highest anthropoid," said the Prof. "Homo sapiens."

That evening, when the circus opened, I couldn't keep track of everything in the crowded tent. The white horses loped around the ring, ladies dancing on their backs in tights and spangles. The ring master in top hat and red tail-coat snapped his whip, a clown with a painted grin and enormous shoes stumbled past us, an acrobat swung from one trapeze to another. The lion and the bear were snarling and pacing up and down their cages and the elephant neatly gathered up the peanuts and popcorn thrown to him by the crowd.

At the far corner of the tent there was a kind of canvas booth and a sign like the one on the toy cart: "Finklemann and Otto, the Talking Monkey. Evolutions's miracle. Admission 25 cents."

The Prof and I wanted to save our money and see the circus again next day so we didn't go into the booth. Hank Dutton did and when he came out we asked him if the monkey talked.

"You can't tell for sure," Hank said. "Mostly chatterin' and squeakin', German, I figger. But that fella's learnin' him. It's worth a quarter all right."

Then I noticed Jessup go into the booth. He stayed there a long while and I wondered why but forgot about him, watching the ring.

It was a great circus and I was full of ice cream and peanuts and tired out by the noise and smelly heat of the tent. The Prof and I had each saved a dollar to see the next day's show and we planned to see the talking monkey, too. But there was no second show.

A pair of strangers arrived in town on the morning train, a burly, tough-looking man with a drooping rusty mustache and his sidekick, a scruffy little fellow with a sour, crooked face. They walked to the rodeo grounds and stayed in the tent for about an hour.

That afternoon we watched the tent come down like a pricked balloon. The rigs and cages were loaded on the special railway cars and the train pulled out for Vancouver late at night.

When I got home from the station I asked Uncle Percy what had happened.

"Creditors," he said. "They distrained the circus for debt. That's the end of it."

But it wasn't the end of it for Jessup and the talking monkey. It was only the beginning.

So far as I remembered, Jessup had never been in the harness room of the livery stable but he was there next day, with Uncle Percy, Hogarth, Brindle, Doc Foster and Tex. From the horse stalls I could see them through the open door.

Otto perched on Jessup's shoulder skinning a banana. While he nibbled it, his eyes, as black and round as buttons, peered about the room and he seemed to be talking quietly to himself. I couldn't make out any words, just squeaks and whimpers. Even without the green uniform he still looked like a dwarf Finklemann.

"So you bought it off that faker." Hogarth was saying. "A hundred dollars fer God's sake and it don't talk."

"Oh yes it does," said Jessup. "A few words already but German, naturally. Finklemann can't speak much English himself. All it needs is more training."

"You expect us to believe that?" Foster demanded. "If any monkey talked we'd of heard of it long ago."

"But it's no ordinary monkey," said Jessup. "It's the first specimen of Ceropithecinae, genus Leuciscus, ever captured by white men in the East Indies. The natives always knew it could talk. In its own language, of course."

Otto was talking fast in its own language and scratching Jessup's head with its slim fingers.

"Curious." Uncle Percy muttered. "And where did Finklemann find it?"

"In Borneo," said Jessup "He barely escaped from the cannibals. Their poisoned arrows ruined his health, I saw the scars— terrible."

"And he put it in the circus?" said Brindle. "A two-bit circus? Why didn't he train the monkey and sell it?"

"He intended to. But Finklemann's an explorer, not a scientist and he lacked the necessary financial resources. Frankly, so do I."

Hogarth spat on the blazing stove. "Yeah, he was broke. The whole damn circus was broke. So he sold you the monkey. But who could train it, even supposin' there was the money?"

"I've made inquiries," Jessup told him. "The Language Institute of Helena, Montana, is equipped for every sort of speech therapy—

the scientific method. And Dr. Hiram Goodacre is undoubtedly the greatest expert in the world."

"Monkey business," Tex growled from his bunk. "You're all loco."

Hogarth paid no attention to him "How much would it cost? How long would it take?"

"That depends," said Jessup. "As you know the simians' laryngeal air sac limits articulation—that is for all species but this one. Minor glottal surgery may be required. Nothing serious."

Hogarth started to pace back and forth across the room. "Never mind that scientific stuff. We'll think about it and let you know."

"Loco, loco" Tex growled again.

Jessup left with Otto on his shoulder.

"He's crazy," said Brindle. "Always was."

Hogarth stopped pacing. "Crazy but honest. And if that monkey can even say howdy-do like a parrot it's worth a million."

Uncle Percy had never liked Jessup but I could see he was getting interested. "Who's this Dr. Hiram Goodacre? And Helena, Montana, of all places? I'll ask Halleck. He may know."

That night Uncle Percy called on Dr. Halleck and came home to read the *Encyclopedia Britannica* and a pile of other books from his shelves. But he said nothing more to me about the monkey. For the next few days the friends in the harness room kept the door closed.

At the print shop Otto usually sat on Jessup's desk, eating bananas and chattering away and peering at the typewriter as Jessup pounded it, or sometimes hanging from a rafter by his tail. The Prof and I began to wonder if maybe he could really learn to talk.

Nobody told us anything but at the end of the week Jessup slipped out of town on the train to the States, taking Otto in a little basket with a cushion to sleep on.

Aunt Minerva soon heard about it and she was furious. "Ha, don't try to fool me!" she shouted at Uncle Percy. "You idiots gave Jessup the money and you'll never see it again."

"A scientific experiment, my dear. If it succeeds..."

"If it succeeds! My land, you expect that monkey to talk? Fiddle-sticks and poppycock! Ninnies the whole kit and boiling of you."

"We shall see."

When Jessup's first telegram arrived I carried it from the rail-way station and read it on the way:

TREATMENT BEGUN GOODACRE CONFIDENT BUT TIME NEEDED.

"How much time?" Hogarth grumbled. "And he'll want more money, that's fer sure."

After another week the second telegram said:

UTTERANCE BECOMING DISTINCT BUT GERMAN STOP MEDICAL FEES HIGH REQUEST FIVE HUNDRED.

"Not a chance," said Hogarth when I brought the telegram to the livery stable.

"Right," Uncle Percy agreed.

"That's only the start." Tex grunted. "He's havin' one hell of a time down there on your money. Loco, loco."

But before the bank of Montreal closed five hundred dollars was wired to Helena.

Still another week passed and then came the third telegram a shocker!

GOODACRE ADVISES MINOR SURGERY VOCAL CORDS SUCCESS ASSURED REMIT FIVE HUNDRED.

Uncle Percy, Hogarth, Brindle and Foster were sitting by the stove and they looked pretty glum.

"It's a gamble," Hogarth said at last "But if it works we'll make a pile."

Brindle turned to Foster, the vet. "What's the risk of surgery?"

"Always risky." said Foster. "But I never operated on monkeys, only horses and cattle and hogs."

After they'd talked for a long while Hogarth walked to the bank

137

and must have wired the money because the next telegram said:

OPERATION SUCCESSFUL RECOVERY SLOW FIVE HUNDRED FOR CONVALESCENCE.

Hogarth's tobacco juice landed on the stove with a hiss. "We're in too deep to get out."

"Indeed," Uncle Percy muttered. "I wish now we hadn't..."

"But we did," said Hogarth. "No, we gotta see it through, win or lose."

The money was wired that afternoon from the bank. After two more days came the bad news.

PATIENT SINKING DUE COMPLICATIONS BUT STILL HOPE RECOVERY.

When I brought the telegram to the harness room Uncle Percy read it aloud.

"Poor little Otto," he said. "We shouldn't have done it."

The others said nothing. They went home and waited.

Every morning and afternoon for the next three days I rode to the station but Lem Brady, the railway agent, had no more message from Helena. On the fourth day I found him listening to his ticker and scribbling on a piece of yellow paper. Over his shoulder I read the words

REGRET PATIENT EXPIRED DECENTLY BURIED AM RETURNING WITH IMPORTANT DISCOVERY.

At the harness room Hogarth crumpled the telegram and threw it into the stove. "Important discovery! A dead cat, a talking monkey and he's dead too! Christ, what next?"

"And all that money," Foster grumbled.

"He's fired," said Brindle. "For good."

"Poor little Otto," Uncle Percy muttered. "And all our fault."

Jessup came back on the train and I met him at the station in our dog-cart. He didn't say a word on the way to the livery stable and kept his valise on his knees as if he thought I might steal it. Uncle

138

Percy and the others were waiting in the harness room.

"So you killed the monkey!" said Hogarth.

Before Jessup could say anything Brindle jumped up and shook his two fists. "Shut up, shut up, you son of a bitch! Fired, fired! Don't ever..."

He slumped into a chair, panting.

Jessup glared back at him through his thick spectacles. "The monkey received the best treatment and I resigned, of course. But that's neither here nor there. All your money will be repaid—with this."

He laid his valise on the table and unlocked it and lifted out a buckskin bag. It was fringed and beaded but old and dirty. Jessup opened the bag and pulled out a little swatch of hair, golden and shiny. "There! From the head of General George Armstrong Custer himself. It's priceless."

Hogarth exploded. "By God, you *are* crazy!"

"Impossible, absurd," Uncle Percy muttered. "The Sioux scalped everybody and kept the scalps."

"But not Custer's," said Jessup. "They didn't touch his scalp and preserved his hair as a brave enemy, a sacred relic. That's well known."

"Hair off of a yallar dog," Tex growled from his bunk. "There's a dozen of 'em on every Injun rancherie"

"And how," asked Uncle Percy, "did you come into possession of the...ah...relic?"

"I was fortunate enough to purchase it at minor cost," said Jessup. "For a song actually."

"And you believed it?"

"Yes, but not till its authenticity was established beyond question. By Sitting Bull."

Uncle Percy's glasses dropped off his nose. "Sitting Bull? He's been dead twenty years."

"True", said Jessup, "but his nephew isn't. He fled to Canada with the Sioux, a young man then. Now he's old, sick, half blind. Works at the Speech Institute, in the garden. Running Wolf he calls himself. But everybody else calls him Joe."

Brindle jumped up again. "Running Wolf? What's he got to do with it?"

"He had the relic. From the Chief himself. And he entrusted it to me."

"Why?" asked Uncle Percy.

"We were friendly. He knew he hadn't long to live and wanted it in safe hands."

"Oh, fer Chrisake!" Hogarth shouted. "Custer, Sitting Bull, Running Wolf! You take us for crazy, too?"

"The proof," said Jessup, "is here."

From the valise he pulled out a strip of wrinkled bucksin. I could see that it had a kind of picture burned on it in rough outline, a bull's head with long horns, crude and faded but a bull's head sure enough.

Jessup waved the buckskin in front of Hogarth's face. "Sitting Bull's own signature. And Custer's hair. Any museum would pay a fortune to get it."

"And if the American government knew you'd taken it there'd be an international incident," said Uncle Percy. "Wars fought for less. But what a tale! We don't even know it's human hair."

"A yallar siwash dog," Tex growled.

Jessup put the beaded bag and the strip of buckskin into his valise. "Very well then. I'll deal with the matter elsewhere. But you'll regret it."

As he started to walk out of the room Uncle Percy stopped him. "Just a moment. You'll consent to a test I presume? A test of the hair, a scientific test, of course. If it's human we can make further studies."

Jessup looked doubtful but in the end he agreed that a sample of the hair, only a few threads, would be sent to the museum in Victoria. Uncle Percy sent it next morning in an envelope by registered mail and everybody waited for a reply from the curator.

"That Runnin' Wolf sells plenty of dog hair, I bet," Tex told me. "Jessup's a bloody idjit."

140

Tex was wrong. After a week the curator wrote that the hair was unquestionably human. When Uncle Percy read the letter to his friends in the harness room Jessup snatched it from his hand and held it up close to his spectacles.

"Human, human! Custer's hair. Now are you satisfied?"

"Not quite," said Uncle Percy. "It might be anyone's."

"But the signature! Sitting Bull's signature, clear as day. It all fits together."

It didn't fit together for long. In a second message the curator wrote that he had neglected to say, in case the question arose, that the human hair had belonged to "a female person, probably of middle age or younger."

"Well, that's it," said Brindle. "He'll never work for me again, never!"

It was a full week before Jessup came back to work. He kept the buckskin bag and Sitting Bull's signature in the drawer of his desk. Now and then he'd take them out and peer at them but nothing about Custer got printed in the *Echo*.

Half-Breed

Dick Lang and I were good friends before his dad was killed by a bullet through the forehead and I guess we still were afterwards, too. No one knew who did the murder and I wasn't even sure if the bullet was fired out of my Winchester .22, not quite anyhow. But everybody said Jim had it coming to him.

I first saw Dick at school and liked him from the start. He was the same age as me, a little smaller but stronger—lean, wiry, and he seemed to move easily and smoothly like a cat. His hair was coal black, his skin dark, though not as dark as an Indian's and his face wasn't Indian, either. Any stranger would have taken him for pure white. But he was half Indian and didn't laugh or talk much except, now and then, to me.

Behind his back the other kids called him a siwash because his mother was a sister of Chief Barnabas. Her real name was Flying Feather but of course she never used it. Everybody called her Rose. She might once have been a good-looking young girl but now her squaw's face was all wrinkled up, most of her teeth missing, her hair dangling in two greasy braids. She spoke pretty fair English with the Indian lisp.

None of the kids dared to say anything about Rose in front of

Dick, not after he'd knocked three of them down and almost choked them for throwing snowballs at her.

The Langs must have been the poorest folks in town. Dick's sweater was out at the elbows and he had only one pair of boots. When they were being repatched at the cobbler's shop he stayed home from school for a couple of days. But he nearly always led our class in the monthly tests and Uncle Percy said he could have made something of himself if he'd got the chance. With a father like Jim and an Indian mother, what chance did he have?

Nobody knew much about Jim Lang, only that he'd come to Emerald Vale before the railway was built and taken up with Rose at Quintlam. Chief Barnabas had no use for him but he made sure that Rose was married by a priest in the little Catholic church on the Reserve just before Dick was born.

"That sonofabitch," I once heard the Chief say to Tex at the livery stable. "One of these days I'll fix him."

"Where I come from" Tex grunted, "we'd of strung the bugger up long ago."

It was easy to talk about fixing Jim but he was too strong for Barnabas or anybody else in town—a big, hulking man with long arms and bulging muscles. His face was blotched from drink, flabby and usually covered with a gray stubble and his knotted hands shook. But he was strong and still a good carpenter when sober. In the early days he'd built a lot of houses around Emerald Vale and even made a fine dining table for Aunt Minerva. With those shaky hands I wondered how he could do it.

"There's mahogany, the real stuff," he told her. "Had it by me ten or twelve years, seasoned right and polished French style. You can't beat mahogany."

Aunt Minerva paid him a hundred dollars and said the table was worth it.

Jim didn't make any more furniture so far as I knew, not even for his own shack, and he was drunk so often or away from town for a month at a time that people stopped hiring him for building jobs.

Once in a while he'd pull himself together, shave and dress in

144

clean clothes and follow Rose to the Catholic church on Sunday. That didn't happen very often and he never built a decent house for her and Dick. They lived in a tar paper shanty at the edge of town and Rose kept them fed by collecting laundry and washing it on a tin board.

Aunt Minerva gave her plenty of warm clothing, cast-off dresses, coats and shoes as good as new, and she wanted me to give Dick some of mine. On a winter day when his bare hands looked blue from the cold I offered him my second pair of wool mitts but he slapped them across my face and walked off and wouldn't speak to me again for a week.

Miss Stella helped Dick by giving him odd jobs around the Majestic with hot grub in the kitchen and more money than he earned.

He's a likely boy," she told me, "but more siwash than white. He could be white, mind you, and go a long ways if they'd let him. But they won't."

Tex helped, too, by paying Dick to water and exercise some of the horses at the livery stable.

"That kid knows hosses," Tex said. "Takes to 'em nacheral like all Injuns."

In the winter Dick and I trapped muskrats in the reeds beside Vermilion Lake and he taught me how to stretch the hides and dry them on a piece of pointed board. We sold them for a quarter each to an old Chinaman who traveled around the country buying up fur from the Indian trappers.

In the spring we sometimes played hooky to fish for trout in the lake with grasshoppers and worms for bait. Uncle Percy had given me his split bamboo rod made in England and Dick would cut a thin willow and tie a line to it. But he generally caught more fish than I did.

"Make sure the spoon works right," he said. "And you're too quick on the strike. Give 'em time to swallow the hook then strike hard." We'd cook the trout on green sticks over our campfire and then I'd feel as Indian as Dick.

145

Uncle Percy had also given me a one-shot Winchester .22 and showed me how to use it to hit a paper target. His own aim must have been better in the South African war. He seldom hit the bull's eye.

"It's only a little rifle," he warned me, "but remember it can kill a man at close range. Never carry it loaded."

I never did and soon learned to shoot pretty well at close range. Dick could hit a tin can on a stump at fifty yards. His arms seemed to be steadier than mine or his eye sharper.

"No," he said, "it's because you jerk the trigger. Don't jerk it, squeeze it, and slow."

After that I squeezed slow and began to shoot better.

Sometimes Dick borrowed the .22 to kill rats swarming around the Langs' shack and sometimes we shot a fool hen perched on a branch. They were out of season in the summer so we didn't bring them home. We plucked and roasted them in the coals of our fire, burning the bones and feathers. The meat was stringy and had no taste, but I guess it made us feel grown-up and tough to be breaking the law and camping under a sheet of canvas.

I didn't dare to ask Dick about Indians, though I wanted to, and he never mentioned his father or mother. But I knew things were getting worse at their shack when Rose came to our house for the laundry with both her eyes swollen and black.

"That man beat her!" cried Aunt Minerva. "I asked her but she wouldn't tell me. I know he beats her. Why doesn't she leave him?"

"Barnabas tried over and over again to take her back to the Reserve with him," said Uncle Percy, "but Rose won't go. She wants to keep the boy in school, to make him white. A sad business, miserable."

"Well, the brute should be locked up."

"Yes, my dear, but what can the police do when she refuses to charge him or give any evidence? Poor soul."

Sergeant Harry Warnock, the only constable of the Provincial Police in the whole Emerald Vale district, was too busy to bother much with drunks. But he often locked Jim in the town jail over-

146

night and let him go next morning. Then he'd disappear for a week or two and come back sober and shaking.

"He's got the horrors," Miss Stella would tell me. "See's things."

"Things?" I said. "What things?"

"Oh, snakes and devils and pink elephants I shouldn't wonder. He's a dipso."

Whenever Jim came staggering and crying into the Majestic Miss Stella refused to let him have any drink but took him to the kitchen and filled him with coffee till he fell asleep in a chair. I think Uncle Percy, or it may have been Sergeant Warnock, asked the second hotel in town, the Plaza, not to sell Jim liquor and the bartender promised he wouldn't.

"They've siwashed him," said Tex. "But it won't do no good. He'll get it anyways."

Jim could get liquor in Kamloops and the other towns and the Indians got it in spite of the law from bootleggers who rode into the Reserve at night and were gone before daylight.

The siwashing of Jim didn't work. Several times Dick came to school with a bruise on his face and I knew his Dad had beaten him. Dick said he'd stumbled in the dark or a horse had kicked him at the livery stable but of course I didn't believe it.

Tex didn't believe it, either.

"Watch that boy," the old man told me while Dick was watering the Clydesdales behind the stable. "Half breeds, you never know what they'll do. Watch him, sonny, he's burnin' inside."

I watched Dick but couldn't see anything different in him. All that summer we fished and shot a few fool hens with my .22 and talked about horses and trout around our campfire, drinking gallons of boiled tea and sleeping sound with one blanket each.

Jim was away for a long time after he'd somehow got hold of a shotgun and blasted out the front windows of the Majestic and gone howling down the street like a coyote and Uncle Percy, as Justice of the Peace sent him to jail in Kamloops. He came back in late August and turned up at the livery stable dressed in clean clothes, shaved and tanned.

Tex shook his hand. "Why, Jim, you're lookin' fine."

"I feel fine," said Jim. "Mighty fine. Lots of grub, lots of exercise. They treated me good."

"Well, jest take it easy now."

"I aim to. Where's Dick?"

"Dunno," Tex lied. "Hasn't been round lately."

Dick was in the yard with the Clydesdales but I saw him hide behind the stable till Jim walked down the street to the Majestic.

"Come on out kid," said Tex. "He's gone."

Dick led the Clydesdales back to their stalls and said nothing.

Miss Stella wouldn't give Jim any liquor and he went over to the Plaza. He didn't get any there, either. But he must have got it somewhere and was drunk and staggering through the streets that afternoon. When Rose brought the week's laundry to our house both her eyes were black and swollen and she had a cut on the chin.

"He's beaten her again," Aunt Minerva told us at dinner. "I asked her but she said she was all right. All right! With that brute? He'll kill her yet."

"If she doesn't kill him first," Uncle Percy muttered. "I sent him to jail for a month and hoped it might teach him a lesson! Apparently not. I'll talk to Barnabas but what can he do if she won't go home to the Reserve?"

After dinner I found Dick in the kitchen of the Majestic eating huckleberry pie. Miss Stella made him take a third piece. "You need to fatten up, boy. You're still too skinny."

"I'm stuffed full," said Dick but the two of us managed to finish the pie and planned to meet early next morning at Vermilion Lake. A new hatch of flying ants should make the trout bite, we figured. I'd ride my cayuse and Dick had a fat old mare from the livery stable because Tex wanted to exercise her.

She carried both of us to our house and it was empty. Aunt Minerva and Aunt Lizzie had gone to Kamloops on a shopping trip, taking Marie along to buy a winter coat. Uncle Percy, I guessed, was at the weekly poker game in the harness room.

Dick borrowed my Winchester to shoot some rats at the Langs' place and rode off. He said he'd bring it to the lake in case we saw any fool hens. I made up a package of sandwiches for our lunch and went to bed.

It was just getting light over the Porcupine Range when I saddled Dock and took the shortcut past Hank Dutton's little spread and the shallow ford across Fury Creek. At the lake I tethered the cayuse so he could fill up on bunch grass and pushed our flat-bottomed punt off the sandy beach.

It was broad daylight now but Dick hadn't come. He still hadn't come after I'd waited about an hour, as I judged the time without a watch, and already there was a rise of trout feeding in the middle of the lake. To hell with him. I got into the punt and rowed toward the rise.

I soon had my troll out and a fish on the hook. It was only about eight inches long but a rainbow by the stripe on its side and I kept it for fear there wouldn't be many others. When I'd caught a second, twice as big, I heard the morning train whistle for the Junction and knew it was now a quarter past nine.

A few minutes later Tex drove his freight wagon along the lake road with hay from Hogarth's ranch. His gray beard was sunk on his chest but he wakened up and yelled at me.

"Any luck, kid?"

I held up my two rainbows.

"Bring me a fat one tonight, eh? They'd go down good."

"Sure," I yelled back. "All you want."

He waved again and the wagon moved into the woods.

The trout were hungrier that morning than I'd ever seen them. In a couple of hours a dozen lay on the floor of the punt, several weighing well over a pound.

The sky had clouded up by now, with thunderheads behind the Range, so I couldn't figure the time but it must have been past noon and I was as hungry as the trout. Nibbling the sandwiches I rowed up and down the lake. Still Dick hadn't come and I thought maybe his father had kept him doing chores at the shack. That was like

149

Jim, the son of a bitch.

It had begun to drizzle and thunder and the first lightning flashed in the south when Dick finally rode out of the woods and waved to me. I rowed half a mile and grounded the punt on the beach.

"What happened, for God's sake?" I said, pretty mad at him.

Dick gave me one of his scowling Indian looks and turned away. "Got hung up."

That was all. No use asking him any more. He tied the mare to a tree and handed me the Winchester.

"You missed the rise," I said. "They won't bite in this thunder,"

"But we might get us a grouse across the lake."

"Not likely and I'm tired rowing. Let's go home."

"I'll row," he said and stepped into the punt.

"Oh, all right."

I sat in the stern with my spoon trailing and the Winchester lying on the floor between Dick's legs. He headed toward the far side of the lake about a mile off where we'd often shot fool hens roosting in the timber.

We were in the middle of the lake when I saw a man ride a big white horse down to the beach and knew it was Sergeant Warnock by his Stetson hat and khaki uniform. He waved and yelled but I couldn't make out his words at this distance.

"What's he want?" I asked Dick. "Must be something wrong."

"Just thinks we're shootin' out of season." Dick said.

With that he picked up the Winchester and before I could stop him had dropped it over the side of the punt.

"Jesus Christ!" I shouted. "That's my gun."

"Best he don't see it. Remember last time he caught us with grouse. Locks us up, he said."

Dick glared at me. I'd seen that look before and it frightened me a little. So I kept quiet and he turned the punt around and headed for the shore.

Sergeant Warnock was waiting for us on the beach—a huge man and a good friend of our family with a square, ruddy face and

150

clipped mustache and usually a smile. But he wasn't smiling now.

"How long you boys been here?" he asked.

"I don't know," I told him. "We've no watch."

"Since about six this morning," Dick said, looking Warnock straight in the eye. "Maybe seven."

I started to contradict him but with that look on his face I said nothing. I was real scared by now. And Warnock's look scared me still more.

"Catch any fish, shoot any grouse?" the sergeant asked.

Dick held up my string of trout. "Plenty of fish, no grouse. We got no gun."

Warnock stooped over the punt and saw there was no gun.

"I've bad news for you, Dick," he said. "Somebody shot your dad a couple of hours ago. He's dead. I'm sorry."

Dick kept looking straight at Warnock.

"Oh," he said.

Warnock frowned back at him. "You wouldn't know anything about the shooting, eh?"

"No, I was here all day."

Warnock turned to me. "That right. He was with you all day?"

I heard myself saying Dick had been with me all day.

"Come on, then," said Warnock. "We better get to town. But mind, Dick, you stay around home. I'll want to talk to you later."

Dick and I got on our horses and Warnock rode close behind us, nobody saying anything. He let Dick turn off the trail to the Langs' shack but followed me to our house.

We found Uncle Percy reading a newspaper on the verandah and Warnock sat down beside him. I unsaddled Dock in the barn and got some grub out of the kitchen cooler and had just started to eat it when Warnock rode off. Uncle Percy took his hat from the hall rack and glanced at me through the kitchen door.

"I'm going to town," he said. "Stay here and don't talk to anyone, not anyone at all. You understand?"

I understood but couldn't bear to stay alone in the empty house thinking about Dick and my Winchester at the bottom of the lake.

After a while I walked to town and saw Uncle Percy's office lighted up behind the curtains drawn across the window. I sneaked through the door from the lane and stood, listening, in the darkness of the back room.

"It's all in the timing."

That was Uncle Percy's voice.

"Shot in the afternoon, not before noon anyways," said Hogarth. "That's what Doc Halleck told Warnock. And it lets young Dick out."

"If he was at the lake early." Brindle grunted. "But was he?"

"Sure he was," said Hogarth. "Percy's boy says so. And then there's Rose. She saw a man with a red beard ride up to the shack with a gun and shoot Jim and ride away before she could stop him."

"Christ, a man with a red beard! In broad daylight?" Brindle muttered. "Who'd believe her? No, they'll pin it on Dick if they can. And if he shot that bastard he did a good job."

"But Warnock has no proof yet," said Uncle Percy. "He's waiting for the inquest."

Then I heard Miss Stella's voice cut in. "Look, we can't handle this thing. Dick needs a good lawyer. He needs Rutledge and I'll pay him no matter what it costs."

"A heap," said Hogarth. "But worth it. Good idea, Stella."

I'd heard of Hammond Rutledge. Everybody had, and I'd often seen his picture in the Vancouver newspapers. He was supposed to be the biggest lawyer in the country, a King's Counsel, whatever that meant. He was always defending someone in court and generally getting them off even if they seemed guilty. It was said he charged as much as $50 a day but of course I couldn't believe that.

Now I heard Hogarth's voice again. "We'll all chip in and I'll wire him tonight."

"I hope he'll come," said Brindle. "He's never failed yet."

There was a scraping of chairs in the front room and I dodged into the lane and walked home before anyone saw me.

The next evening, when Rutledge arrived on the Vancouver

152

train, I barely recognized him from his picture. He was bent almost double, with rheumatism I supposed. Each of his hands, like a crooked claw, held a thick wooden cane. Slowly, inch by inch, he eased himself down to the platform and stood blowing and swaying, his face twisted with pain. It was a face you'd remember— long, hollow, deeply grooved. A mass of snow white hair sprawled from under his floppy black hat. He seemed unable to raise his head, even when Hogarth grabbed his arm to steady him.

"Thank you, sir. Thank you. Mr. Hogarth, I presume?"

The voice sounded like treacle, just as the newspapers always described it, but they never mentioned that he was a cripple.

Hogarth almost had to lift him into the front seat of the Reo and lift him out at the door of the Majestic. Miss Stella had fixed her two best rooms for him on the ground floor so he wouldn't have to climb any stairs. She'd also fixed a special dinner in another room and he ate it there with Hogarth, Uncle Percy and Brindle so they could talk about the murder, I guessed.

Uncle Percy had told me to be in his office at nine that night. When I got there Rutledge was slumped nearly flat in a leather armchair, his legs stretched out in front of him, his white hair brushed up into a kind of plume. Only his eyes moved, blue and hard as agates under the shaggy brows.

"Well, young man," he began in his treacle voice, "tell me what happened at the lake. What time did your friend Dick arrive?"

"I had no watch," I said, avoiding his eyes. My hands were damp and my stomach churning.

"But you could tell the time, more or less, by the sun?"

"It was cloudy. I never saw the sun."

"Just so. Did he come early?"

"I didn't notice."

"It was before noon?"

"I think so."

"You think so. But you're not sure?"

"It was before noon."

"And you'll tell that to the coroner—on oath?"

"Yes," I gulped.

He stared at me for quite a while. "Not very satisfactory," he said. "You can go now. But don't talk to anyone."

I scurried through the front door in a muck sweat.

Next morning Hogarth drove Rutledge down to Quintlam in the Reo. Dick and Rose were staying there with Chief Barnabas. I didn't hear what Rutledge found out but in the afternoon I saw him hobble on his two canes into Sergeant Warnock's office beside the jail and then Hogarth took him to the livery stable.

After that he called at the Gem Grocery and must have talked for half an hour in the back room with Peter Jardine who called himself "The Particular Grocer" and had just been appointed Coroner of Emerald Vale. Jardine was a scrawny, shrunken man too small for his clothes with a face the color of putty, a long neck like a plucked rooster and a pair of gold-rimmed glasses pinched on his sharp nose. He knew nothing about the law and hadn't yet held an inquest but he worked hard for the Conservative Party at election time and the Government in Victoria wanted to keep him working.

The inquest on Jim Lang was to be held in the old court house, built before the railway, its outside log walls now covered with shingles, the inside with pine boards. When Uncle Percy took me there the main room was full already.

Jardine sat at the raised judges' desk, in his Sunday suit and high starched collar, his putty face screwed up behind the gold-rimmed glasses and looking important. To his right six men, the jury I supposed, were back of a railing—Ben Stott, the Fire Chief, his black beard cut square, his frock coat too tight for his belly, his white shirt front bulging, Frank Dutton in fringed and beaded buckskin, Doc Foster's little goat whisker wagging on his chin. I didn't know the other three men.

To Jardine's left Hammond Rutledge hunched over a table, his nose almost touching it. Sergeant Warnock was with him, bolt upright in khaki uniform.

Uncle Percy and I squeezed into the last row of benches beside Miss Stella and Hogarth.

154

"There's nothing to be afraid of," she whispered and patted my knee. But I was terrified and sweating in the hot little room with its smell of new pine boards.

Now, in the front row, I saw Barnabas, Rose and Dick huddled together but I couldn't see their faces.

After it was all over I didn't remember much about the inquest—only Jardine polishing his glasses on a handkerchief and nodding and muttering from time to time, the jurymen paying no attention to him, Dr. Halleck kissing the Bible and saying that Jim had died around three o'clock, at the earliest, and Warnock telling how he had talked to Dick and me at the lake.

Then Rose stood up, wearing one of Aunt Minerva's dresses, her eyes still swollen, her face wrinkled and stolid. I could barely hear the words as she said in her lisping Indian voice that she'd seen a big man with a red beard and a gun ride into the yard and shoot Jim through the window of his workshop and gallop away. But I was sure nobody believed her.

I could barely hear Dick, either, when Jardine handed him the Bible. He touched it to his lips and stared straight in front of him, his face blank as if he didn't see the coroner or the jury.

Jardine cleared his throat with a gurgling sound. "What time did you leave for the lake?"

"Early," Dick said.

"Yes, yes, I see. How early?"

"I don't know. But it was just getting light."

Ben Stott leaned against the railing and thrust out his square beard.

"Did you shoot your father?" he demanded.

"No," said Dick. "I was at the lake."

"I see, I see," Jardine muttered. "At the lake early. That's important."

I wondered if the jury believed Dick and I wondered why Rutledge had said nothing. He didn't seem to be interested.

Miss Stella stretched across me to Uncle Percy.

"Why doesn't he do something?" she whispered.

Uncle Percy shook his head. I could tell he was worried.

When Jardine called me I could hardly stumble down the aisle. All I remember now is Jardine's putty face, Dick watching me with those blank eyes and Barnabas's silver teeth glistening.

"What time did Dick come to the lake?" Jardine asked me.

"I had no watch," I mumbled.

"Before noon?" said Ben.

"Long before noon."

"Before nine, maybe?"

"About nine, I guess."

"About nine," said Jardine. "I see, I see. That's important. Any more questions?"

Nobody asked any more questions and I stumbled back to the bench. Miss Stella patted my knee again. "Good boy," she whispered. But Uncle Percy said nothing.

It was only then that Rutledge lurched from his chair, panting and shuffling. Crouched over the table, he twisted his head sideways, trying to look up at Jardine.

"If it please Your Honor," he began in that purring tone, "I appear amicus curiae, a friend of the court, the usual procedure, you understand."

I could tell that Jardine didn't understand at all, and neither did I, but he bobbed his head and polished his glasses. "Yes yes, I see. Of course, Mr. Rutledge, of course."

"Thank you, sir. Now then, one point at least, I submit, is clear, the vital time factor, as I'm sure this intelligent jury will agree."

He glanced at the jurymen sideways and they nodded.

"Just so," he went on. "But regarding that point you may assume, quite naturally, that Rose Lang, the mother, and Dick, the son, are perhaps confused by such a tragic event. Certainly they had no special affection for the deceased—a fact well understood among you for obvious reasons. Doubt, therefore, may arise. However..."

He paused, glaring up at Jardine from under his bushy eyebrows.

156

"However, there is an additional witness and with Your Honor's permission I shall now call Mr. Cornelius Dodd, better known, I believe, as Texas. He's waiting outside."

My heart seemed to bump against my ribs. Tex had seen me in the punt that morning, seen me alone. All Dick's lies, and mine, were no more use now. I wanted to slink away and hide somewhere.

Everybody turned toward the open door. Old Tex came slouching down the aisle in a clean blue shirt and a new pair of overall pants. Even his beard looked clean. He raised the Bible to his lips and stood facing Jardine. Warnock's mouth had fallen open. Nobody could have warned him about Tex. The jurymen all leaned against their rail. Jardine was muttering and polishing his glasses.

Rutledge kept his hands pressed on the table and twisted his head sideways at Tex.

"Now then, Mr. Dodd," he said, "just tell us, in your own words, what you saw, if anything, on the day of Jim Lang's death."

"Well, it wasn't much," said Tex. "I come along the lake with a load of hay and I seen the two boys fishin' in a boat and I talked to 'em. That's all."

"Quite so, Mr. Dodd, quite so. And what time was that?"

"Quarter past nine it was."

"But how could you be sure? Did you consult your watch?"

"No, but I heard the train whistlin' fer the Junction and I seen the smoke over the trees."

My heart stopped thumping. That old devil, Tex.

Rutledge twisted his head toward Jardine. "If necessary, Your Honor, we can call the station agent to testify as to whether the train was on time."

"Not necessary," said Jardine. "I was at the station myself that morning. The train was right on time."

"Very well, Your Honor. If there are no further questions, I suggest, with respect, that the evidence is complete and no doubt the jury will wish to consider it."

"Yes, yes, the evidence," Jardine muttered. "The jury will consider the evidence."

The jurymen filed into the room at the back of the courthouse. Tex sat down beside Barnabas. Dick was looking straight ahead, his face still blank. Rose's eyes were closed tight but her lips moved and I guessed she was praying.

Miss Stella patted my knee again. "It's all right," she whispered. I hoped so but wasn't sure. Would the jury believe Tex?

In about five minutes the jurymen filed in behind their rail. Ben Stott pulled a slip of paper out of his vest pocket and squinted at it.

"We find," he said, "that Jim Lang come to his death from a bullet fired by persons unknown, so help us, God."

Afterwards, in the crowd outside, I couldn't see Barnabas or Rose and Dick. They'd disappeared and so had Tex.

Hogarth and Uncle Percy helped Rutledge struggle into the Reo. He slumped in the front seat, panting.

"But surely," I heard Uncle Percy saying, "they can still charge the boy even now?"

For the first time Rutledge seemed to be grinning. "On that evidence? No, no, they'll never charge him. Not against Tex's accurate memory. The case is closed."

"Thanks to you," said Uncle Percy.

"Thanks to Cornelius Dodd. A remarkable old man that, very."

He grinned under those shaggy eyebrows. "Besides, my clients are always innocent."

Then Hogarth drove him off to the Majestic.

I wanted to talk the whole thing over with Dick and next day I rode down to Quintlam. But they told me there that Barnabas had driven his wagon to his brother's place on the Fountain Reserve near Lillooet and taken Rose and Dick with him. I never saw my friend again.

Three Fishers

The whole thing started, I guess, when Uncle Percy bought the gramophone by mail order from Eaton's in Toronto. It had a black horn and a brown wooden box with the machinery inside. The records were little wax cylinders that fitted a metal roller. They would play for a couple of minutes if you wound up the handle tight.

Of course I'd known about Irene Blake long before the gramophone arrived. Everybody did. Her pictures were often in the newspapers and they called her the Canadian Melba. I didn't know anything about Melba and I hadn't heard Blake sing till Uncle Percy lifted the gramophone out of the packing case and set it on a table in the parlor.

"It's an ugly thing," said Aunt Minerva. "Hideous. Does it work?"

Uncle Percy wound the handle and slipped a record onto the roller. "Wait, my dear. I've a treat for you."

At first there was only the scratching of the needle but in a moment you might have thought someone was playing a piano here in the room. Then came a voice and I'll never forget it—soft and high like a woman's and suddenly deep and low like a man's.

I'll never forget the words either.

"Three fishers went sailing away to the west, away to the west as the sun went down and the harbor bar was moaning."

I could almost see them in their little boat and hear the gurgle of the sea. And at the end the three drowned bodies on the shining beach, the women weeping and wringing their hands.

"...the sooner it's over the sooner to sleep and good-bye to the bar and its moaning, moan-ning."

That voice. It sent a tingle down my spine.

Aunt Minerva had listened without a word till the needle began to scratch again.

"It's her," she muttered. "It's Gertie."

"No, no, Irene Blake," said Uncle Percy. "Unmistakable."

"She'll always be Gertie to me."

"What! You knew her?"

"Ha, did I know her? My land, we were chums at the music school together, the Toronto conservatory—Gertrude Skulason. But we called her Gertie. And oh, how she could sing even in those days."

Uncle Percy twisted the points of his mustache. "And now she's Irene Blake. I don't understand."

Aunt Minerva giggled. "We got the names out of the telephone book. She couldn't sing, professionally, I mean, with her real name. Imagine Skulason on a program. It's Icelandic."

"Icelandic? She was from Iceland?"

"From some town in Manitoba—immigrants all of them. But good people, fishermen, I think they were."

"Fishermen, eh? No wonder she could sing that song. She feels it."

"Gertie could sing anything, any note from soprano to contralto. A freak voice like Melba's. Play it again."

Uncle Percy cranked the gramophone and we listened to that voice and the moaning of the harbor bar. My throat felt chokey.

"A marvelous invention," said Uncle Percy and he lifted the needle off the record.

162

Aunt Minerva was staring out the window. "It misses her range, her *color*. Gertie was such a big girl, not pretty but tall and strong as a man, and funny, too. She glowed, she just *glowed*. And how she worked on her voice! The rest of us dropped out, one by one. But I stood up with Gertie at the wedding. In a church vestry it was. They couldn't afford a proper wedding."

"She's married? The papers never mention any husband."

"No, he's gone, years ago. But that was Tony you heard at the piano. He always accompanied her. Tony Spencer, I'd know his touch anywhere."

"Wait a minute," said Uncle Percy. "Gertrude something or other, then Irene Blake and now Mrs. Tony Spencer? Well, really! And what happened to him?"

"Who knows? They were too young, just kids. And Tony so moody, so sensitive. Jealous of her, maybe. Or maybe there was another woman. Or another man. They'd traveled all over the States and Europe, everywhere. But he disappeared. Poor Tony."

Uncle Percy grinned. "Why, I believe you were in love with the fellow yourself!"

"All of us were, a little. He was so handsome, so tall, so nice to everybody. But then you came along."

Uncle Percy grinned again. "So you had all the luck, my dear."

"Fiddlesticks! I wonder where he can be? And Gertie. The last letter I had, she was in Vienna, or was it Rome? I've a mind to write her, for old time's sake. She's near fifty if she's a day."

"Doesn't sound like it on the record," said Uncle Percy. "But of course it might be an old one."

"Must be, with Tony at the piano. And yet it seems only yesterday."

"Time passes. Still write to her by all means. She's in Montreal getting ready for a tour of Canada. I read it in the papers. A farewell tour."

"Farewell? Ha, she'll sing till she drops."

"No doubt. And now, perhaps, something more cheerful? The latest thing from New York, I understand."

He cranked the gramophone and put another record on the roller. There was a rumble of drums and the hoarse blare of a man's voice.

"Come out and hear, come out and hear Alexander's ragtime band..."

Aunt Minerva jumped up from her chair. "You call that music? Turn it off, turn it off!"

He left the record going to the end in spite of her and I began to think he liked it. I liked it fine anyway, the song and the band, without knowing what ragtime meant. Afterwards, whenever I was alone in the house I often played the record and learned all the words and sang them out loud with the gramophone. But I never played "The Three Fishers." I didn't want to think about them or hear that woman's voice.

Easter came early, about a month after we'd got the gramophone, the spring chilly, the first green bunchgrass on the foothills.

Marie was a good cook but she couldn't learn to make hot-cross buns, so I drove Aunt Minerva to Fritz Heinrich's bake shop. His buns were the best ever baked outside England, Uncle Percy always said.

I stayed in the dog-cart and Aunt Minerva went into the shop. While I waited, cold and cranky, a man rode down the main street, a stranger to me but I recognized his mare, a clumsy old chestnut from Hank Dutton's place on Fury Creek, her coat still thick and shaggy, her ribs showing from a winter on the range.

Thinking of those hot-cross buns, I didn't pay any attention to the stranger when he tied the mare to the hitching post in front of the shop. All I noticed was that he wore a checked red mackinaw and looked tall and stooped. A sickly man, as lean and clumsy as the mare.

He was opening the door of the shop as Aunt Minerva walked out, her arms full of parcels. They bumped into each other and one of the paper bags fell to the sidewalk.

"Can't you see where you're going?" she spluttered.

"I beg your pardon," said the stranger and picked up the bag and handed it to her.

She turned away but stopped and peered up into his face.

"My land, I do believe! No, it couldn't be..."

She turned away again but he held her arm "Great God, it's Min!"

I'd never heard anyone call her Min and for a moment she just gaped at him.

"Tony!"

All the parcels dropped and she was hugging him.

Tony Spencer, the piano player, didn't look like the man Aunt Minerva had told us about. He wasn't handsome or nice, his cheeks white and pinched, his straggly black beard flecked with gray.

They were still clinging together, both talking at once.

"How'd you get here, Tony? Why here? What's happened to you?"

"Nothing much," he said. "Taking a holiday, wandering around. Doctor's orders, the dry air.."

"You're ill?"

"No, tired, that's all. And how did *you* get here, Min?"

"Oh, I've been here for ages."

He smiled down at her. "Married, too, I'll bet."

"Yes, and my name's Archer."

"Well, well, congratulations, Mrs. Archer."

"Nonsense! But what are you doing, Tony? Where are you staying?"

"I rented a little cabin for the summer. From the Duttons. You know them?"

"Of course I know them. But alone in a cabin? And your music?"

"No piano," he said. "I don't miss it."

"You don't miss it? Ha, a likely story. And what about..."

Aunt Minerva stopped, her face reddened and she turned to me.

"Boy, you ride that horse. I'll take Mr. Spencer in the cart."

"But Min," he said. "I can't..."

"Oh yes you can. You're coming home for dinner. I declare you look starved. Get in, get in."

I jumped from the cart and they got in. Aunt Minerva shook the reins and drove off.

Well now, I thought, this is a queer howdy-do but I rode home slowly on the old chestnut mare and hitched her to the fence behind the kitchen and brought her a bucket of oats from the barn.

In the parlor I found Uncle Percy and Aunt Minerva sitting by the open fire, Tony between them. He'd taken off his red mackinaw and wore a blue wool sweater. There was a tumbler in his hand and Uncle Percy held one too. A faint tinge of color had come into Tony's cheeks and all of them were laughing at some joke.

Uncle Percy refilled the two tumblers from a bottle and glanced toward the mahogany piano in the corner. "Minerva used to play, played very well. But she's given it up. Rather a pity. I suppose you wouldn't care to..."

"No thanks," said Tony. "I've forgotten how."

Aunt Minerva slapped his knee. "Forgotten! Rubbish! You'll never forget, never."

By this time I was mighty hungry and went into the kitchen for a snack. Marie said her chicken and apple pie would soon be cooked but I ate a couple of hot-cross buns to keep me going. As I was starting on another I heard the tinkle of the piano. Strange, I thought, Aunt Minerva playing again after all these years.

But when I opened the parlor door Tony was hunched over the piano, his fingers running along the keys. Long fingers, I saw now, long and thin, and each seemed to have a life of its own.

Aunt Minerva and Uncle Percy hadn't noticed me, their eyes fixed on Tony.

I stood still, the bun halfway to my mouth. That music, it sounded different from any I'd ever heard, even from the gramophone—sometimes soft and slow, then fast and sharp. It reminded me of a bubbling mountain stream, rain pattering on aspen leaves, the clink of breaking spring ice, all kinds of things that made no sense. Marie peeked through the doorway, her head

166

bobbing.

Tony's hands fell from the keys. It was a full minute before anyone spoke.

"I knew it," Aunt Minerva whispered. "I knew it."

"A pretty tune," said Uncle Percy.

Aunt Minerva glared at him. "A pretty tune? You call that a tune, the "Moonlight Sonata?" Ha, if Beethoven could hear you!"

"He'd only laugh," said Tony and laughed himself.

Dinner was late, the chicken overcooked, the pie crust burned, Marie fidgeting and mumbling in French. But Tony seemed to fancy the grub. He ate a lot of the chicken and a big slab of the pie.

In the parlor Uncle Percy stoked up the fire. Aunt Minerva and Tony sat in front of it with their coffee.

"Good to have you here, Spencer," said Uncle Percy. "You'll like it, once the weather warms up. And now perhaps..."

He glanced at Aunt Minerva and she nodded. Fumbling among the records, he put one of them on the roller and cranked the gramophone. The needle scratched and then the voice of Irene Blake pealed out.

"Three fishers went sailing away to the west, away to the west as the sun went down..."

That voice again, the three drowned men on the sand. I felt all choked up.

Aunt Minerva was watching Tony. He didn't move but the cup shook in his hand and some of the coffee spilled on the hearth.

"...and goodbye to the bar and its moaning, moan-ning."

Tony laid the cup on the table. He started to speak but broke off and stood looking out the window. Behind him I saw the moon just above the Porcupine Range, as yellow and round as a Cheddar cheese. Then, before anyone could say a word, he walked through the front door and unhitched the mare and swung into the saddle.

"Don't try to stop him!" cried Aunt Minerva. "Let him go, let him go!"

Tony had gone already down the road.

"For God's sake," Uncle Percy muttered. "What's that mean?"

Aunt Minerva snorted. "It means he still loves her of course. He wants her, you ninny. But he'll be back, oh yes, he'll be back."

I was surprised to see her smiling.

"A rum business," said Uncle Percy. "And he forgot to take his coat."

Tony didn't come back for a couple of weeks and then only because Aunt Minerva drove out, alone in the dog-cart, to his cabin beside Fury Creek. What she said to him I never heard but one night, early in May, he rode to our house on the chestnut mare.

This time he was dressed in city clothes, a brown tweed suit, shirt and tie. He'd shaved off that straggly beard and looked younger than I first thought—about Aunt Minerva's age. His face was getting sunburned and not so pinched and drawn.

When we finished dinner he played the piano again, without glancing at the keys. Nobody mentioned Gertie all evening and Aunt Minerva had stowed the gramophone in the attic. But as Tony rode off in the dark Uncle Percy said, "He's on the mend. He's getting over it. The dry air, the exercise."

"Oh, you ninny," said Aunt Minerva.

After that, Tony came every week, on Sunday nights, looking better and eating more and playing longer every time. He knew a lot of music besides sonatas and the classical stuff, even some of the tunes from *The Merry Widow* I'd heard on the gramophone. Best of all Uncle Percy liked the songs from Gilbert and Sullivan, especially *The Mikado* and *H.M.S. Pinafore*. I liked them fine, too, and soon learned the words. We'd join in the chorus while Marie giggled from the kitchen doorway.

One night, Tony stopped playing and grinned at Aunt Minerva. "Listen to this, Min. You'll love it." He started to hammer the keys, his shoulders heaving, and I knew the tune right away.

"Come out and hear," he whooped in a twanging Yankee voice, "come out and hear, Alexander's ragtime band..."

Aunt Minerva pretended to put her fingers in her ears but Tony sang the song to the finish.

"You always had a vulgar streak," she said.

168

"And you were always a snob, Min. Uppity."

"What's wrong with it?" Uncle Percy demanded. "Capital song, capital. The Americans are good at that kind of thing."

Lucky, I thought, Aunt Lizzie was in the east or she'd have a conniption fit and bust her corsets.

Aunt Minerva had warned me not to talk about Tony around town and I didn't. But in the long evenings I'd often ride out to his cabin on Fury Creek and he seemed glad to see me. It must have been lonely for him, with the Duttons on the prairies visiting Susan's folks and no neighbors within miles.

Sometimes we'd sit by the creek and he'd tell me funny stories about his travels in Europe but he never spoke about Gertie and I never asked him. Sometimes we'd ride on Hogarth's range, the clumsy chestnut lumbering and blowing behind my little cayuse. Tony was learning to ride pretty well by now and I taught him how to troll for trout from the leaky punt on Vermilion Lake. Then we'd cook them on green willow sticks over a fire on the beach and eat them with our fingers.

"Food for the gods," he'd say. "Ambrosia. This is the life my lad."

I couldn't quite make him out but we got to be good friends and I was sorry to hear he'd be leaving in the fall for a job with some orchestra in the States.

One day early in June when I picked up our mail at the Post Office I noticed a letter from Montreal and brought it home with the rest. Aunt Minerva stopped polishing the piano and opened the envelope and read the letter twice, her lips moving, her eyes popping.

"My land! Oh, my land!"

"What's happened?" I said.

"Later, boy, later. Run along now."

She folded the letter and shoved it into the pocket of her skirt. But at dinner she told us that Irene Blake was going to sing in Kamloops next week and had invited her to the concert.

"That's nice," said Uncle Percy. "Of course you must go."

169

"Yes, but I wonder if I'll recognize Gertie? And she'll hardly know me."

"Nonsense, my dear. You haven't changed a bit."

When Aunt Minerva arrived back from Kamloops on the afternoon train I met her at the station with the dog-cart. I'd never seen her in such a tizzy but she wouldn't tell me anything on the way home. It wasn't till dinner time that I heard the news.

"Gertie's coming," she cried before Uncle Percy was even through the front door.

"What! You mean she's coming here? To the Vale? When?"

"On Saturday. It's all fixed."

"But not to sing? Not in this town?"

"Yes, to sing. And we've only four days to get the hall ready tickets, decorations, everything."

Uncle Percy sank into a chair. "Does Tony know?"

"Not yet but he'll find out soon enough."

"I hope not." He looked hard at Aunt Minerva over his glasses. "You know what I think? I think you persuaded her..."

"Ha, think as you please, there's work to do."

There sure was. Next morning Aunt Minerva called a meeting of the Ladies' Choral Society in our parlor and they decided to hold the concert outdoors. Brindle headed a committee to clean up the rodeo grounds and collect all the wooden benches he could find. A headline across the front page of the *Echo* said EMERALD VALE WELCOMES CANADA'S MELBA. Underneath, a blurred photo of Gertie must have been taken years ago when she was young. She'd look different now, I guessed. Uncle Percy sold tickets like hot cakes at his office, a dollar apiece, to cover expenses with nothing for Gertie. The whole town was buzzing and they kept me busy, too, running errands.

I thought of riding to Fury Creek and telling Tony about the concert but what was the use? He'd hear anyway and I knew he'd stay out there till Gertie left.

She came on the Friday afternoon train from Vancouver. Only a small crowd waited at the station and nobody cheered or clapped as she stepped down to the platform. We just stared.

I wouldn't have known her by the photo in the paper. She was tall, big in the chest, big all over, too big for her black dress. Under the yellow hair, coiled in a braid around her head, Gertie's face was plump, smooth and ruddy like a girl's, like a ripe peach. But when she smiled I noticed the wrinkles around her eyes, the bluest I'd ever seen. And I noticed something else. Aunt Minerva had told us this woman glowed. I hadn't believed it at the time but now I did. There was no other word for it—she *glowed*.

Before I could make up my mind whether she was pretty or homely Aunt Minerva hugged her, both of them half laughing and half crying.

"Welcome, Miss Blake," said Uncle Percy. "We're honored."

She shook his hand. "Mr. Archer? No, I'll call you Percy."

Her voice was clear and soft but nothing special, not the strong voice on the gramophone. Maybe, I thought, it's worn out. This was supposed to be her farewell tour.

Uncle Percy glanced past her to the Pullman car. "You're alone?"

"Yes. My accompanist fell sick in Vancouver last night. I had to come without him."

Aunt Minerva was leading her across the platform. "Don't fret, Gertie. We've got quite a good pianist in town. He'll do with a little rehearsing."

"You mean Keevil?" said Uncle Percy. "He's hardly..."

"He'll do," Aunt Minerva snapped.

I didn't think he'd do at all—Howard Keevil, that dried-out shriveled-up little music teacher always wriggling and sniffling at the piano. But it was none of my business.

Gertie took my hand. "So you're Min's boy?" She had a grip like a man's.

I mumbled something and gathered up her two suitcases and carried them to Miss Stella's Reo behind the platform. Hogarth sat at the wheel, mighty nervous.

He slid out and opened the door for Gertie and Aunt Minerva.

They climbed into the back seat. Uncle Percy sat with Hogarth and the Reo went clanking and smoking down the street.

I rode my cayuse out of town. Uncle Percy had asked me to see if everything was fixed at the rodeo grounds and it seemed to be.

The platform was draped in bunting, red white and blue. A couple of men were putting benches around it on the grass. A sheet covered the grand piano. The Union Jack hung limp from the flag-pole. The sky was cloudless in the twilight and I guessed there'd be no rain tomorrow.

It was too late for dinner by the time I got home but Marie always kept some grub hot for me. I'd just settled the cayuse down for the night with hay and oats when I saw Keevil getting into his buggy at the front steps. He never liked me after I quit his piano class and I didn't like him, either. But I said good night anyway and asked how the rehearsal with Gertie had gone.

"What's that to you?" he grumbled.

I couldn't see his face in the darkness, only the high white collar and long cuffs.

"Nothing," I said.

"Nothing to you! Nothing to her! No time to practice. New music, new songs. All mad, stark mad."

He was still muttering as the buggy creaked out of the yard.

Everybody else had gone to bed but Marie gave me a pile of meat and vegetables in the kitchen. Her fat cheeks were quivering.

"*Quelle chanteuse*! What a singer! *Mon Dieu,* the house shakes, the windows rattle. But *gentil*, that one, *très gentil.*"

Next morning we were all up early. At breakfast Aunt Minerva told us she was taking Gertie for a drive to see the country around the Vale.

"Nice day for a picnic," said Uncle Percy. "And relaxing before the concert."

Gertie laughed. "Relaxing? Why Percy, you'd think this was my first appearance."

She ate more breakfast than any of us.

"That's an extraordinary woman," said Uncle Percy after Gertie

172

and Aunt Minerva had driven off in the dog-cart. "No nerves, no temperament, no side to her. And a voice like a whole orchestra. Extraordinary."

I saddled the cayuse and found Brindle in his shirt sleeves at the rodeo grounds, fussing like a broody hen but stopping to gaze up at the sky. Tex was helping some men unload extra benches from his freight wagon.

"Forget it, Mike," he said. "No chance of rain. But this singer, can she sing?"

Brindle wiped his bald head with a handkerchief. "Christ, I hope so. It'll be the biggest crowd we ever had, bigger than Laurier's, bigger than Borden's, bigger than McBride's even."

By noon all the benches were in place. More bunting had been nailed to the platform, the sheet stripped off the grand piano, and it glinted in the sun.

Brindle heaved himself up to the seat beside Tex and the wagon trundled through the open double gate.

I had plenty to do all that afternoon carrying messages between town and the rodeo grounds. By six o'clock the first rigs and saddle horses were hitched to the trees outside the fence. Inside, a few people slouched on the benches eating sandwiches and drinking pop. After the special train arrived from Kamloops all the benches filled up and more people streamed through the gate. I watched to see if Tony was among them but he wasn't. Lucky, I thought.

An hour before the concert would start I figured the crowd at five hundred, maybe a thousand, but I was too hot to count them. Faint puffs of wind brought the smell of sagebrush and alkali, stinging and bitter, off the foothills. I kept my eye on the road, waiting for Hogarth and the Reo with Gertie, Aunt Minerva and Uncle Percy. There was no sign of them, no word from our house and by eight o'clock I began to think something must have gone wrong.

The crowd was quiet but getting restless, everybody watching the gate. Beside the platform steps Keevil clutched a roll of papers, music I guessed. His tiny face was screwed up tight and he shivered in his frock coat. Brindle paced back and forth, stopping every minute to peer at his watch.

I slipped into a bench next to Miss Stella, Tex and Doc Foster.

"Hour late already," Tex grunted. "Where's the damn singer?"

"She'll be here soon," I said.

"By God, she'd better or else..."

"Look!" cried Miss Stella and pointed down the road. I saw the whirl of dust and heard the chug-chug of the Reo. It came sputtering past the gate to the end of the platform. Everybody was standing and clapping.

I couldn't make out what had happened till Gertie mounted the steps. She was wrapped in a black cloak but she threw it across the grand piano and turned to smile and wave at the crowd. Her long dress glistened silvery in the twilight, the yellow hair rippled around her bare shoulders.

Nobody clapped any more. The crowd stood there without a sound just looking at her. It was true all right. This big woman glowed.

Now Uncle Percy was in front of the platform, mighty fine with his cream-colored linen suit, and Aunt Minerva with her green Sunday silk.

"Ladies and gentlemen," he began, "I know you will excuse this delay through circumstances beyond...ah...our guest's control. But happy circumstances, I may say. She will be accompanied tonight by her husband, Mr. Anthony Spencer..."

The crowd's murmur drowned the rest of his speech.

Miss Stella squeezed my arm. "Her *husband*?"

"That fella Tony!" said Foster. "A piano player? I don't believe it."

"It's him for sure," Tex muttered. "But can he play?"

Tony was climbing the steps and now I guessed the whole thing—the drive in the dog-cart, the picnic in the country, that devilish aunt of mine. She'd even fooled Uncle Percy.

On the platform Tony bowed and sat down at the piano. He was mighty fine, too, in full evening clothes, white shirt and all. On their benches the crowd was so quiet I could hear the rustle of harness and a horse whinny outside the fence.

Tony's fingers ran slowly along the keys. Then Gertie's voice, soft and low but rising sharp and clear like a trumpet and ending in a kind of sigh, a whisper. The words were foreign. The crowd hardly clapped at all.

"Eyetalian," Tex grunted. "Dago."

"No, German," said Foster.

Gertie was smiling. She didn't care what the crowd thought.

At her nod the piano tinkled like sleigh bells in the winter time. Of course everybody knew the second tune.

"The sun shines bright on my old Kentucky home..."

Gertie's voice had changed. She might have been singing a lullaby and rocking a cradle.

When the last notes faded everybody was clapping.

Foster clapped with the others, his beard wagging. "That's the stuff."

"Yeah, she sings pretty good," said Tex.

Gertie whispered something to Tony. He struck a single crashing note and a different voice boomed out.

"Land of hope and glory, mother of the free..."

A gale in the forest, a rumble of thunder, a throb of drums. That sounds crazy now but so I heard it.

"...God who made thee mighty make thee mightier yet."

Uncle Percy jumped up waving his straw hat and yelling, "bravo, bravo!" The whole crowd yelled with him.

I expected Gertie to be gasping for breath but she was smiling at the crowd again and Tony smiled, too.

After that, I don't remember much about the concert. There were a lot more songs, some of them foreign, some sad, some light and funny, even "a bicycle built for two", and when she sang in a rasping cockney accent "wontcher buy me jellied eels in Picca-dilly?" she had us laughing fit to bust.

But at the end of "Love's Old Sweet Song" tears rolled down Miss Stella's cheeks. I was feeling a little choked up myself.

The thin sliver of a new moon had edged above the Porcupine

Range but I couldn't see Gertie's face, only the glisten of the dress and the white patch of Tony's shirt.

She was bending and whispering to him. As he struck the first notes on the piano I knew what was coming. The "Moonlight Sonata" floated out, seemed to linger on the air and drift into the hills.

In the dead hush that followed Uncle Percy stood before the platform. "Ladies, and gentlemen, this concludes, fittingly indeed, Irene Blake's ...ah...Mrs. Spencer's magnificent..."

But he didn't finish. The crowd was on its feet shouting "more! more! encore! encore!"

Gertie raised her hand and everybody settled back into the benches.

"Thank you," she said in her ordinary voice. "We both thank you. And I'll sing an old, old song I used to sing long, long ago."

The piano tinkled and for the first time she stretched out her arms as if to touch us. Now the voice I knew so well and yet so much clearer and stronger than the gramophone record.

"Three fishers went sailing away to the west, away to the west as the sun went down..."

I saw it all, the little boat crossing the harbor bar, the storm, the drowned men on the shining sand, the women weeping and wringing their hands.

"...there's little to earn and many to keep and good-bye to the bar and its moaning, moaning, mo-aning."

At the end no one stirred for quite a while. Then everybody was clapping and clamoring below the platform. Gertie bowed low in a kind of curtsey and Tony bowed with her, their arms around each other. But I blubbered like a baby.

When we got to the station, after midnight, it was jammed and the heads of the passengers hung through the windows of the special train.

On the steps of the last car Gertie and Tony were hugging Aunt Minerva.

Uncle Percy had said goodbye already and stood aside with me,

176

his linen suit rumpled and soiled, his straw hat missing.

"A rum business," he muttered. "Extraordinary woman, that. Extraordinary both of them. Who'd have thought..."

I heard the conductor yell "all aboard," the engine bell clanged, the crowd let out a final cheer, the train jerked and started to move down the track.

Aunt Minerva was still waving a handkerchief as the lights disappeared around the bend.

Whisky Jack

Ever since I was a little boy, Roland Trickett had come out from England and spent a summer month with us. The air of the Dry Belt, he said, helped him breathe. Even here he couldn't breathe without puffing and gurgling and thumping his chest. Then he'd clear his throat, relight his pipe and talk by the hour in a funny accent of his own. It seemed to have a touch of cockney in it and he'd slur the words together, starting most of his sentences with "yem, yem" and "gar, gar." Or so it sounded to me.

We were all used to his queer ways but I guess we never really knew him till the riot at the Whisky Jack mine.

By that time Trickett must have been very old, at least sixty, but he had no wife or any relatives that I'd ever heard of. He was short and square and chunky. Sometimes his face reminded me of an angry bulldog and sometimes of a baby's. When he laughed two dimples flickered in his pink cheeks. The white line cutting across the bristles of reddish hair on his head was from a bullet in the South African war but it hadn't done him much harm. What made him wheeze and gasp was a second bullet through the lung.

"He was too old to be there at all," Uncle Percy told me. "But they let him go as a correspondent from some London paper and I first met him when we relieved Ladysmith. Oh, Trick was a mad chap in those days. Wouldn't stay behind the lines, kept right up with us, wandered all over the place. Mad, mad. But his dispatches were brilliant, not like his talk. That other newspaper fellow, Churchill was good, too, and went into politics. But as good as Trick? No!"

Uncle Percy always called him Trick but Aunt Minerva called him Roly Poly and he called her the Hell Cat and often hugged her like a clumsy bear. "God Almighty," he'd shout. "She's just as happy as if she had good sense."

I was old enough to know that with all his fooling around Trickett said little about his own life. So far as I could make out from Uncle Percy he was born poor in London and worked on ocean liners and in the mines of Colorado and Nevada. Somehow he'd got into the newspaper business and travelled all over the world.

"He's been everywhere, seen everything, and written about it," Uncle Percy said. "You won't see anyone like Trick again, my boy."

"Ha, there's more to it," said Aunt Minerva. "Something happened, a woman most likely. But we'll never hear it from old Roly Poly."

When he arrived on the train, that year of the riot, and lurched down to the station platform he wore his usual rough tweed suit in spite of the heat and carried a heavy valise in one hand and a thick, knobbly cane in the other.

"God Almighty!" he bellowed. "What a trip, what a country, what am I doin' here? And is this the Hell Cat I see before my dyin' eyes? Buss me, then, buss me, you lovely, lovely creature!"

After he hugged Aunt Minerva and shook Uncle Percy's hand and patted my head we drove him to the house in the dog-cart and settled him in the spare room for a nap. But he soon stumbled downstairs to ask if next day was Marie's day off. When Aunt Minerva said it was, he refused a lift and walked alone to town, for exercise, he said. Of course we all knew what was coming.

At the butcher shop he ordered mutton chops, as he did every year. "Only chump chops, mind," he said and stood by Ben Stott to

180

make sure they were real chump chops, not lamb, and cut an inch thick.

Next morning he fried them, sweating, honking and drooling over the kitchen stove. Aunt Minerva and Aunt Lizzie tried to help him but he drove them from the kitchen. "Away with your janglin' and jonglin', you monstrous regiment of women," he howled, "And if I leave don't think I won't take my chops with me."

My aunts fled, even Lizzie tittering.

Eventually he served up the breakfast, so much of it that I couldn't eat all mine. One day he finished his last hunk of greasy mutton and scowled at us like a bulldog. "Man is a carnivore. Therefore he will fight, red in tooth and claw. And the big war's comin' never fear."

"In this day and age?" said Uncle Percy.' "I can't believe it, Trick."

"You can't eh? Gar, you still believe in progress? Even you. Progress, what's progress? Only the inflammation of some bloody historian's gall bladder."

"Roly Poly," cried Aunt Minerva, "you're impossible."

His face took on the baby look. "True, true. And oh how you love me, darlin' Hell Cat!"

Every morning, after breakfast, he'd light his pipe and set out for town, pockets bulging with extra pipes and a big tobacco pouch, his knobbly cane tapping on the wooden sidewalks. He peered into the store windows, yarned with Brindle about newspapers at the *Echo* office or sat with Tex in the harness room, both of them smoking their smelly pipes and talking about horses.

Just before lunch he usually took Uncle Percy to the Majestic for a drink and stopped at the desk in the lobby to tell Miss Stella that she was looking more gorgeous all the time. She said he was an old fool but I think she liked it.

In the bar Uncle Percy drank scotch, Trickett always rum mixed with lime juice. Through the open window I once saw him hold the glass against the sunlight and mutter, "Scotch for boys, brandy for Napoleon. But rum for heroes. That's why we beat him at Waterloo." He sipped the rum slowly, laughing, wheezing and gurgling.

On Saturdays a locomotive brought five or six flat cars full of coal from the Whisky Jack and took them north to Kamloops. The mine was only about three miles from the Vale but after one look I never rode there again.

The Whisky Jack village was much smaller and even worse than Copper Ridge—a gaping hole in the side of a cliff, bony horses dragging little cars on tracks out of the tunnel and, further down the hill, the miners' shanties, all solid black with coal dust.

The dust smeared everything, the bare ground, the faces of the miners, the laundry on the clotheslines. A few men from the night's graveyard shift were sitting in front of the shanties but they didn't look up at me as I rode past. Some women leaned over steaming tubs on the porches or lugged bags of groceries from the grimy store, their heads covered with shawls.

There were only about two hundred people at the Whisky Jack, all of them too poor and beat, I guess, to complain. But only a mile or so away the owner of the mine lived in a big white house beside a lawn, trees and flowers.

His name was Derrick Croft, a giant of a man with a face hard as granite, a trailing mustache and bloodshot eyes. He'd come from somewhere in the States and bought the coal vein from Lucky Murphy who'd found it long before the railway was built to Kamloops. Murphy was supposed to have named the vein for one of those sassy gray birds that lived in the hills and stole food out of his frying pan. No one knew how much money Croft had paid him but Lucky soon got rid of it and died in the Kamloops old men's home.

Everybody around the Vale seemed to hate Croft. He didn't care and seldom came to town unless he was taking the train to the coast. I guessed he must be very rich and he often brought one of his nieces back with him from Seattle.

"Nieces?" said Aunt Minerva. "Ha, *nieces*! That awful man. As if..."

"Now, now, mind your language before the young." Trickett

wheezed. "And he's a great man of business, a family man devoted to his nieces, an upstanding citizen of the glorious American republic."

Trickett's laugh ended in a gurgle and a fit of coughing.

On Saturdays about a dozen miners rode the flat cars of coal to town and lounged in the streets, all of them dressed the same, in ragged caps and coats, scarves around their necks and string tied around their pants below the knees. After the night shift they must have washed themselves in those tin tubs I'd seen at the Whisky Jack. Their faces were clean but pale from lack of sun, I guessed.

People called them Fifers because they came from some place with a name like that in Scotland and they had a strange accent. I could hardly understand it but Trickett understood it fine. He would sit on the edge of the sidewalk, puffing his pipe and talking to them, sometimes for hours, and often buying them beer at the Majestic. They couldn't buy much themselves on their wages of $3 a day for ten hours of work.

All the miners took to Trickett but he talked mostly to a man who wasn't like the Fifers and spoke like a Yankee, with a kind of foreign twist. His name was Sam Lowe. Everybody called him Little Sammy. He was only about five feet high and under a shock of fiery red hair his hollow face was sprinkled with bluish pits. There were more pits on his hands and a dent in his forehead. Trickett said he'd been through a mine explosion in the States but Little Sammy never mentioned it to me.

Passing him and Trickett as they lolled on the sidewalk, I caught snatches of their talk, words like "stope", "winze", and "stull" and I didn't know what they meant. But I remembered that Trickett had worked in the mines and figured that he and Sammy had plenty to yarn about.

One Saturday, when the Fifers had walked home to the Whisky Jack, Trickett strolled over to the livery stable and sank down in his usual chair.

"Quite a card, that Sammy. I can't make him out," he wheezed.

"Well, I can," said Hogarth. "He's one of them sea lawyers,

stirrin' up trouble. A dangerous fella, and a foreigner, too, by the looks of him. From Russia or Germany or somewheres, with a fake Yankee name."

Trickett shoved tobacco into his pipe and scowled at Hogarth. "He's just a miner, a working stiff. But he'd read a few books and started thinkin', that's all. So did I at his age. Gar, I was a bloody communist. Sammy dangerous? Rot and twaddle."

"A rough diamond but harmless," Uncle Percy agreed. "A decent chap I always thought. And who'd want to work for Croft? That swine."

"But he pays their wages," said Brindle.

Trickett got his pipe going and fanned the smoke away from his face. "What wages! And that a mine!"

"Sure, he's tight with money," said Hogarth "but there's nothin' wrong with the mine."

Trickett scowled at him again. "Everything's wrong with it. Bad timberin', weak stulls, not enough pillars. All run on the cheap. The Whisky Jack's a bloody death trap."

"Huh, you been listenin' to Sammy," said Hogarth. "That rebel, that socialist. Why Christ, you talk like a socialist yourself."

Trickett stumbled to his feet and grinned, the dimples showing in his cheeks. "I was, too, until I got some sense. And now for a rum ration, the drinks on me."

They all walked to the Majestic but only Trickett ordered rum. The others drank scotch or rye.

On the night before Trickett was to leave for England Marie served his favorite dinner of roast beef, undercooked and dripping blood, with crisp Yorkshire pudding. By the time Trickett had eaten three helpings his face looked almost as red as the beef and gravy had dripped on his vest.

"A dinner fit for a king," he wheezed. "Gar, too good for him. Marie, my love, you're an artist. French, poor soul, but an artist."

Marie blushed and giggled.

Trickett's bag had been packed, he'd said good-bye to his friends, given Miss Stella a smacking kiss and Sammy a dozen cases of

184

beer for the Fifers. His train was due to pull out at eight o'clock next morning so we all went to bed early.

Full of roast beef, I slept sound and didn't even hear the phone ring or any noise on the stairs. But toward dawn the sputter of the Reo woke me up. Jumping out of bed, I ran to the window and in the half light saw Uncle Percy and Trickett climb into the seat beside Hogarth. The Reo clanked off, a trail of smoke behind it.

When I got downstairs Aunt Minerva was standing at the front door in her nighty.

"What's wrong?" I asked.

"An accident," she said. "At the mine. That's all we've heard. Now go back to bed."

Of course I wouldn't go back to bed. Neither would Aunt Minerva. She put on her dressing gown, lighted the stove and made some coffee and we waited in the kitchen. It seemed a long time before the sun came up. Marie cooked breakfast, jabbering and moaning to herself in French. Aunt Minerva phoned Brindle and Miss Stella but nobody had heard any more from the Whisky Jack, only that there'd been an accident.

It was almost noon and I was getting hungry again when the Reo chugged into the yard. Uncle Percy, Trickett and Hogarth climbed out, their faces and clothes black with coal dust.

Aunt Minerva met them at the front door. "My land, what's happened?" But she kept her head and made them sit down at the kitchen table and poured three cups of coffee.

"And a drop of whisky," Uncle Percy muttered. "We need it."

"Better than nothing," said Trickett. He rubbed his face with a handkerchief and it was smeared black.

"A hell of a thing," was all Hogarth could say.

Aunt Minverva found a bottle in the cupboard and splashed whisky into three glasses. The men all drank it neat. I was busting to ask about the mine but for quite a while they said nothing more.

After they'd drunk the rest of the whisky, Trickett began to fill his pipe. He couldn't do it and was coughing and thumping his chest so hard I thought he'd strangle.

"Take it easy", said Aunt Minerva. "Don't try to talk."

"A hell of a thing," Hogarth grunted again.

It came out, bit by bit, though I couldn't understand it very well at the time—the fall of rock on the night shift, five men buried, one crawling from the tunnel but so badly hurt that they brought him in the Reo to the Vale Hospital. Dr. Halleck had cut off both his legs above the knees and thought he might live. Little Sammy and the day shift were still trying to dig through the slide with picks and shovels.

"Hopeless," Uncle Percy muttered. "And those women, the children and Croft away in Seattle."

"Sonofabitch," said Hogarth.

Trickett had managed to light his pipe at last. "Now then, God, stand up in the witness box," he wheezed, "and let's hear what you've got to say for yourself."

The train had left hours ago but Trickett didn't seem to mind. That afternoon he sent a telegram to London and settled into the spare room.

Two days later, Croft came back to town and brought a steam shovel on a flat car from Kamloops and a crew of six men to run it.

The rock was soon cleared from the tunnel and I heard that the dead miners, what was left of them, had been reburied in the cemetery downhill from the mine. Uncle Percy and his friends went to the funeral but he wouldn't talk about it and I didn't want to know.

No more coal was mined at the Whisky Jack. The Fifers had gone on strike for an eight-hour day, wages of $4 and a lot of changes in the mine that I couldn't understand. The men in the harness room talked about them with Little Sammy but through the open door I could only make out that some of the pillars and timbering had broken and the roof caved in.

"Bound to happen sooner or later," Trickett was saying. "A wonder it didn't explode."

"We told him," said Sammy. "Told him over and over again but he wouldn't listen."

186

Trickett dragged a notebook and a pencil from his coat pocket. "By God, we'll make him listen."

While the others sat watching him he laid the notebook on the table and began to scribble in it. I heard the pencil scraping the paper and Trickett's gurgles but didn't know what he was writing till he finished and thrust the pencil back into his pocket.

Hogarth stopped pacing across the room. "You writin' him a letter, Trick? That won't help any."

"A few vague notions for Brindle and the *Echo* to chew on," said Trickett. "A judicious editorial—mild, too mild. Here, read it, Mike."

Brindle picked up the notebook and began to read aloud.

"Mr. Derrick Croft is not on trial in the courts today only because the law fails to provide a condign punishment for his crime of greed, neglect and vaulting megalomania. But when the coal baron of Whisky Jack prefers his profits to human life the higher court of public opinion will judge his deep damnation..."

"Christ," Brindle muttered, "that's pretty rough."

"Go on," said Trickett, "read it."

Brindle's putty cheeks turned crimson and his chins trembled as he kept reading, but I can't remember much except the last sentence.

"A man who gorges on the toil and misery and even the lives of his workers has no body, parts or passion."

Hogarth's fist pounded the table. "Right, jest right! It's a beaut."

"Too strong perhaps," said Uncle Percy and even Little Sammy shook his head.

Brindle handed the notebook to Trickett. "Libelous, libelous as hell. Croft'll sue me, ruin me and the paper. No, no."

"Libelous?" said Trickett. "Of course. But you think he'll sue before a jury of his peers in Emerald Vale? Rot! The bastard's not crazy. Go ahead and print it. Make the *Echo* ring? Gar, light your candle in a naughty world and it'll listen."

"No, no," Brindle sputtered. "It might do in London, not in this town. I can't print it."

187

Trickett glowered at him. "Well then, rewrite it to suit yourself. Squeeze the juice out of it. But you'll wish you hadn't."

"No, no, I can't," Brindle said again. "Impossible."

When they'd talked for another half hour Brindle suddenly ripped some pages from the notebook and stuffed them into his pocket. "All right, I'll do it. So help me, I'll do it."

The next issue of the *Echo*, three days later, carried the editorial in big print on the front page. So far as I could see not a word had been changed. I didn't quite understand the last sentence about body, parts and passion but it sounded terrific.

About dusk that same night Uncle Percy and his friends had just left the Majestic bar and stood on the steps under the flickering new electric sign when Croft rolled up the street in his buggy, his pair of matched grays steaming. At the corner he jumped down to the sidewalk, a copy of the *Echo* in one hand and a thick cane in the other. He looked to be steaming as hard as the grays.

From the opposite side of the street I watched him limp toward the hotel and remembered he had a game leg. He had a swollen belly, too, but he was as strong as a horse and over six feet tall. His face, half hidden by a floppy sombrero, might have been roughly hacked out of stone and left unfinished.

"You sonofabitch!" he yelled, waving the paper in front of Brindle. "Lies, lies! Libel! I'll sue the ass off you, I'll break you..."

In the glow of the electric sign I could see him puffing through his long black mustache.

Then he noticed Trickett and shoved Brindle aside.

"You wrote that stuff! Brindle couldn't, not him. You goddamn limey, you...why you goddamn socialist, you communist..."

"You goddamn capitalist," said Trickett. He leaned on his own cane staring up at Croft. "And a bloody fool, too. Just wait till they sue *you* for damages. Gar, they'll break your bloody mine."

Croft's cheeks bulged and the mustache fluttered again. "Break me? Those measly Fifers? Huh, I'll show you who'll break."

"Really now," said Uncle Percy but Croft wasn't listening. As he swung his cane at Trickett I saw Hogarth grab it and throw it on the sidewalk. "Beat it, Croft! Out, out, sue and be damned!"

Croft seemed to hesitate but after a moment he stooped down and picked up his cane. "You'll be hearin' from my lawyers." He limped to the buggy and drove off.

From the doorway of the hotel Miss Stella waved her hand. "Bye, bye, baby. Write home when you get work."

Trickett beamed at her, wheezing and coughing. "Aha, you young she-devil! But he's not finished yet. Yem, yem, we'll hear from him."

"And then what?" Brindle muttered. "Sue me? I wish to God we hadn't..."

"Naw, naw," said Hogarth. "Not a chance." He turned to Trickett. "But the Fifers can't sue him, can they? You're only bluffin' and he knows it."

"Bluffin' of course," Trickett wheezed. "And so was Croft. He won't dare sue and the miners couldn't prove anything. Oh no, he kept within the law. A cunning bastard. I know his kind—all bluff, no bottom. He's losin' too much on the mine, he's got to start it workin' and he'll break."

Croft didn't break. The mine tunnel was clear but a sign at the mouth said

PRIVATE PROPERTY TRESPASSERS PROSECUTED.

The Fifers stayed away from the mine and one night they met in the school yard to form a union with Little Sammy heading it. But the union was no help to them. Their families would have gone hungry, I guessed, if it hadn't been for a committee set up in the harness room with Uncle Percy as chairman. He and Trickett and Hogarth bustled around town, asking the storekeepers to give the Fifers some credit, and most of them did. Everybody thought Croft's wages of $3 a day were mean, the working shift of ten hours too long, the mine dangerous.

Aunt Minerva, Aunt Lizzie and Marie made hampers of grub and more of them came from Miss Stella's kitchen in the Majestic. Hogarth took the hampers to the Whisky Jack village in the Reo. I think he gave the women some money as well but he never talked about it.

After a month the strike was still on. Croft didn't come to town any more and I heard he was denned up in his house with one of his nieces and a couple of Chinese flunkies.

When school opened in the fall I began to wonder if the mine would ever re-open. But in the harness room Trickett kept telling the others that Croft would soon break.

"God, I hope so," said Brindle. "The strike's awful bad for business. I can't stand it much longer."

"Croft's rich, loaded," Tex growled from his bunk. "What's he care?"

"He cares about money," said Trickett. "That's all he cares about. Just wait. Yem, yem, he'll break."

Hogarth spat on the cold stove. "We'll wait but the Fifers? No jobs, no wages, nowhere else to go. They can't wait. And that Sammy. Where's he bin? Never seen hide nor hair of him. He's up to somethin' you can bet."

"Only talk," said Trickett. "They'll wait."

He and his friends heard nothing more till the day of the riot and then it was too late to stop the Fifers.

When the Reo rumbled out of town that afternoon I figured something was going to happen and I followed on my cayuse. By the time I got to the Whisky Jack the parade had started.

Everybody from the village seemed to be marching up the road, Little Sammy in front, behind him another man pounding a big drum and another blowing a bagpipe. After them came five long wooden boxes of rough lumber draped in black cloth, each carried on the shoulders of two men. I could see that the boxes were empty but they looked enough like coffins to remind Croft of the men buried in his mine.

A few of the Fifers toted placards nailed to sticks. The crude lettering said "Starvation Wages," "No More Murders," "Safety or Profits?"

The rest of the marchers straggled in a swaying line, men,

190

women and kids in their tattered clothes, all singing a kind of chant. The drum and the bagpipe made such a racket that I couldn't hear any words and the alkali dust from the road stung my eyes. But I knew where the parade was going all right. Croft's house was set in a grove of poplars on the far side of the naked sagebrush hill.

Hogarth knew, too. He edged the Reo off the road, past the parade and caught up with Sammy. Through the dust I saw Trickett clamber down, waving his cane and shouting. Uncle Percy stood in the Reo with Hogarth and Brindle.

The parade had stopped and so had the drum and bagpipe. Even in the hush I couldn't make out what Trickett was saying to Sammy. But after a minute or two they trudged up the hill together, the drum beat, the bagpipe squealed and the parade lurched along with me still at the tail end.

Over the top of the hill the road went down in steep zig-zags. Sammy and Trickett cut across them through the sagebrush. The Reo kept to the curves and I passed it at a gallop. "Get back! Get back!" Uncle Percy yelled but I pretended not to hear him and slowed to a trot.

The road wound through the poplars to the edge of Croft's garden and on to his sprawling white house. As Sammy and Trickett started up the gravel driveway the line of the parade broke. Everybody ran over the lawn and flower beds, howling. I galloped ahead and saw Trickett pound his fist on the front door. It swung open and Croft stood there in his shirt sleeves, a rifle in his hands. At the sight of it the howling faltered.

Now I heard Trickett's voice. "Drop that gun!"

"One step," said Croft, "and I'll shoot."

Sammy reached for the rifle but Trickett's cane cut him across the arm. "Don't be a bloody fool, Sammy," He turned to Croft. "Drop that gun! Drop it."

Croft shoved the muzzle against Trickett's chest. "Get your mob off my place! And quick about it."

Trickett didn't move. Croft was blowing through his mustache and I thought the rifle shook in his hands. Sammy rubbed his arm but said nothing. The face of a young woman peered through a window and then she was gone. Two Chinamen in white aprons scampered from the side of the house and into the trees.

"Christ, the bastard means it," said Hogarth.

"Come away, Trick, come away!" Uncle Percy shouted.

The Fifers had started howling again and pressed closer to the steps. The women ran out of the garden and dragged their kids with them.

In all the din I couldn't hear what Croft was saying. But suddenly he lowered the rifle and Trickett and Sammy followed him into the house. The door closed behind them. The crowd fell silent and waited. Most of them lounged on the grass, some on the empty coffin boxes, the drummer on his drum.

Uncle Percy polished his spectacles with a handkerchief. "I don't like it. Not that gun."

"But he didn't shoot," said Hogarth. "Trick was right. Croft'll break."

"What if he don't?" Brindle muttered.

Half an hour must have passed but it seemed longer. The women and kids straggled back and sat down beside the men. My cayuse was restless, chewing his bit and pawing the grass. I patted his neck and quieted him.

At last the door opened. Everybody jumped up. Trickett came out, Sammy next and then Croft without the rifle.

Sammy was grinning and I thought Croft was almost grinning, too.

Trickett raised both hands above his head. "Ladies and gentlemen, your attention please. Mr. Croft has agreed to certain terms. Tell 'em Sammy."

"It's like this," Sammy began. "Wages four dollars, nine hours..."

"And new safety rules," said Trickett. "Satisfactory to a miners' committee. Right, Mr. Croft?"

Croft wasn't grinning any more but he nodded and mumbled

192

something under his mustache.

Trickett raised his hands again. "How about that my friends?"

Everybody was laughing and cheering. The drum beat and the bagpipe squealed.

"By God he's done it!" Hogarth shouted. "Trick's done it!"

"Let's get out of here," Brindle muttered.

The Fifers lifted Sammy on their shoulders and carried him down the driveway. Trickett watched them go, still grinning. I was surprised to see him shake Croft's hand before he walked over to the Reo.

Croft stood on the porch, wagging his head. Then he went into the house and closed the door behind him.

Now the crowd was moving up the hill, the drum beating, the bagpipe squealing, the coffin boxes and placards left scattered beside the driveway.

Trickett settled into the front seat of the Reo and thumped his chest "Yem, yem, I told you he'd break. Gar, all bluster, no bottom. And he was losin' too much money. So that ends it."

But it hadn't quite ended.

The night before Trickett was to leave for England I drove to town in the dog-cart to bring him and Uncle Percy home. They were with Hogarth and Brindle on the steps of the Majestic under the flickering electric sign.

I'd just reined in the colt when Croft's team of grays came tearing along the street. At the corner he scrambled down from the buggy and limped to the steps.

Trickett was the first to speak. "Well, Mr. Croft?"

"You welshin' on the deal?" said Hogarth.

Croft scowled at him. "Never welshed in my life. Huh, the deal's goin' to bust me. But there's somethin' else I forgot up at the house."

He towered above Trickett, blowing through his mustache. "Your goddamn editorial! That's what!"

"We've been over it already," said Trickett. "The subject is closed."

"Nothin' personal," Brindle sputtered.

Croft's eyes bulged out. "Nothin' personal? So I've got no body parts or passion eh?"

"A figure of speech," said Uncle Percy.

Trickett looked up at Croft a queer little smile dimpling his cheeks. "So that's it. My, my. A question of honor."

"A goddamn insult!" Croft yelled and shook his cane in Trickett's face. "Dirty, dirty, below the belt. Take it back! Take it back!"

"On reflection," said Trickett, "I think you have a point. Below the belt, yem, yem. And inaccurate, too, obviously inaccurate in your case."

"You take it back?"

"The personal reference. But no more."

Croft lowered his cane. He was really grinning now and in the electric light I could see his big yellow teeth bared. "Good enough. I'll take your apology. Forget the rest, it don't signify. All lies but only business. Huh, this calls for a drink, a last drink before you leave town, you goddamn limey."

Nobody spoke for a moment, everybody's eyes on Croft as if they couldn't believe him.

"Very well," said Trickett. "One drink with the busted coal baron won't do us any harm. One drink and I don't have to like him."

Croft was still blowing through his mustache and for the first time I heard him laugh. "Come on, boys, no hard feelin's, only business."

All of them walked up the steps and into the bar. It was a full hour before they came out and I saw there'd been a lot more than one drink.

Croft shook the other men's hands, one by one, and limped to the corner, weaving from side to side. But he managed to climb into his buggy and the grays started off at a slow trot.

Hogarth alone looked fairly sober. He left Brindle sitting on the steps and took Uncle Percy and Trickett by the arms and led them across the street. I helped them into the dog-cart.

As I drove home Uncle Percy's head was sunk on his chest and

194

he seemed to be dozing. Trickett kept trying to light his pipe but couldn't get it going.

"Rum for heroes," he mumbled. And after a while, "Percy, you've got a wonderful little town. Yem, yem, crazy but wonderful."

Aunt Minerva was waiting at the front door of the house.

"My land!" she cried. "You're a disgrace. Both of you a disgrace!"

Trickett's clumsy hand patted her cheek. "And you, lovely creature, you're a Hell Cat."

Next morning we put him on the train and watched him wave his cane from the back platform.

A few months later Uncle Percy read the obituary in the London Times. It said Trickett had been "a major journalist, a master of his craft."

"Poor Roly Poly," Aunt Minerva whispered. Tears oozed from her eyes and Uncle Percy dabbed his own with a handkerchief. I didn't feel like crying but I always remembered Trickett's words on that last night. Emerald Vale, yes, a crazy, wonderful little town.

Homecoming

Since I'd left it in my youth for the university in Toronto I never saw Emerald Vale again until my seventieth year. Then it was a mistake to return. After a pretty strenuous life in distant cities and foreign lands, I should have known better. I should have known that everything I'd once been was as dead as my wife, uncle, aunt and all my boyhood friends. But an old man's curiosity, the special vice of my newspaper trade, and perhaps a twitch of doting nostalgia, the vice of every old man, pulled me back to the Dry Belt for one last look.

On a hot summer morning I drove out of Kamloops, my favorite grandson and namesake, David, beside me. At his age of fifteen he was an ordinary boy, raised in Victoria and distinguished only by his skill in violent athletic sports and his mop of straw-colored hair, wildly overgrown, though expensively trimmed in the latest fashion.

To him the scenery was strange but the broad, paved highway, with its teeming traffic, must have seemed natural. To me it was unnatural, almost unbelievable. At my age, of course, nothing lives up to a man's expectations, or his memories.

"How far?" David kept asking. It was near lunchtime and even a gigantic breakfast in the Kamloops hotel could not sustain him much longer.

"We'll be there in an hour, or less," I said and held the speedometer around 80 kilometers. "Then a hamburger, maybe, and a coke? As many as you want."

"That's super, Gramp. But was it always hot like this in the olden days?"

"Always hot. And cold in winter. You get used to it."

He gazed over the empty range, the few green pockets of irrigation along the river bank and the tractors working in the alfalfa fields. "I thought it'd be different. I thought there'd be lots of horses."

Obviously the Dry Belt had disappointed him. My disappointment was sharper but I didn't try to explain it. The generation gap is a jaded newspaper cliché but happens to be true.

At the river crossing, the narrow wooden bridge was gone and in its place stood a wide span of glistening metal. On the far side the little houses of the red light district were gone, too, superseded by a shopping mall, vast and hideous. Red lights of another sort flashed at the street corners.

Traffic lights in Emerald Vale! On this street where the only horseless vehicle I ever saw was Dandy Ryan's crimson Reo. I hadn't expected horses and wagons but the swarm of automobiles and trucks surprised me. As I'd been warned, a big pulp mill, ten miles out of town, spread its fumes of prosperity across the range when the wind blew from the west. So it was blowing today and prickling my nostrils.

"Jeez, what a stink!" said David.

But the inhabitants, I guessed, were hardened to the money smell and didn't miss the whiff of sagebrush and alkali.

When we squeezed past a green light and turned the next corner I saw that the Majestic had somehow escaped the tide of progress, the inflammation, as Trickett called it, of some liberal historian's gall bladder.

The hotel stood in the familiar place, the electric sign above it,

198

but the clapboard walls, painted white and often repainted in Miss Stella's time, were covered with imitation shingles of brown felt, some torn and flapping loose. The bar room was a squalid coffee shop—no bar, none of Fritz Heinrich's gorgeous murals, only plastic tables and chairs and a couple of waitresses looking more painted than clean.

"Don't let's eat in that crummy joint," said David.

The Majestic was crummy all right and I stopped in front of it less than a minute. Further down the street we found a parking meter (a parking meter instead of a hitching post!) and left the car there.

By now I'd almost lost my way among the new stores, offices, hotels and a movie theatre with a chromium facade and a life-size picture of Marlon Brando playing *The Godfather*. (A fine actor, but he couldn't have played Louis Riel as Uncle Percy had played him.)

And where was Uncle Percy's office? It had disappeared from its corner to make room for a glass and concrete tower five stories high. The livery stable, Tex's pungent kingdom, had become a garage, a showroom full of automobiles and a parking lot with half a dozen gas pumps.

But the Emporium was hardly changed at all, except for the misshapen furniture, the television sets and women's underwear behind the window instead of the crockery, cheap jewelry, saddles, spurs and harness that I used to admire and envy. As I peered at these modern improvements David plucked my arm. "Gramp, I'm hungry. Aren't you?"

"Yes," I said, lying. "We'll find a good place to eat right away."

We couldn't find a good place but the restaurant was clean, the hamburgers edible. David quickly consumed three of them while I nibbled one and left most of it uneaten.

Afterwards, I inquired my way to the *Echo*, hoping to glance at its early files, if they still existed. In a neat front office, too neat and shiny for my taste, the stout, bejeweled dragon lady at the counter told me that the files, and everything else, had been burned long before she came to town. Mike Brindle? She'd heard the name and thought he was once the editor. But why did I ask?

I didn't inform her. What was the use? How could anyone explain that Brindle's ponderous editorials had carried some of the authentic frontier tang? And doubtless I was the only man still alive who remembered Uncle Percy's great scoop on the death of King Edward, or Jessup's fillers promoting a world revolution, or Trickett's indictment of Croft's body parts and passion— all glorious stuff to me, to me alone.

The *Echo*'s latest edition filled twelve pages of excellent offset typography, syndicated pictures and cartoons and a big headline announcing the construction of a new City Hall. But this was a faint echo of a metropolitan paper. It had no tang.

I left the office without giving my name and bought David a triple ice cream cone to soothe his impatience. In a flower shop I bought myself an armful of hot-house roses, their price outrageous.

At the sight of them David snickered. "You got a girl friend in town, Gramp?"

"Several," I told him, "and none of your damn business."

"Boy, oh boy," he said.

When we got back to the car he asked where we were going.

"You'll see," I said and knew exactly where we were going. But Uncle Percy's house was no longer at the edge of town. Flimsy bungalows surrounded it, gray stucco had been plastered over the red bricks, fake Tudor beams nailed across the gables.

I stopped the car by the concrete sidewalk and read the brass sign at the front door—Ye Olde English Inn.

"What's this joint?" said David.

I couldn't bear to tell him and muttered that I'd once lived here.

"In this dump? It's gross."

So it was. Gross, debauched, pitiable. Lucky, I thought, that Uncle Percy and Aunt Minerva wouldn't see it.

I saw it through a blur of memories—the fire I'd set in Sir John's bed, Aunt Minerva mopping up the water from the firemen's hose, Gertie singing "The Three Fishers", the wedding breakfast for

200

Miss Stella and Hogarth, Uncle Percy's toast to the bride in champagne punch, then a lengthy speech on the menace of German militarism and Laurier's tin-pot navy, while Aunt Lizzy, ignorant of the alcoholic content, drank freely, murmuring "delish punsh", and snored gently in her chair.

Memories, and mine alone, too deep for tears, but I must have been crying all the same.

"Anything wrong, Gramp?" David asked.

"Only a speck of dust in my eye," I said, and rubbed it with a handkerchief.

Better he shouldn't hear about the last days of our family in this house. I'd heard little myself when my job was based in London and Uncle Percy's infrequent letters told me nothing of his troubles, the loss of all his money in some mining deal. The debts that ended his business.

It was a long time before I learned that Aunt Minerva had taken in boarders, cooking their meals herself, Uncle Percy as handyman and gardener. I did what I could to help but, with troubles of my own, it didn't amount to much. The news of their deaths, each within a year of the other, reached me in Paris and then I began to realize what I owed them. Too late for regrets, too deep for tears.

"Jeez, it's hot," David grumbled. "Let's get out of here."

"One more thing," I said and drove up the street.

It took only a few minutes to pass the last houses and climb the hill east of town, the hill we had slowly climbed in our sleigh for Dandy Ryan's funeral. The graveyard was almost empty then, under deep snow. Now the graves huddled together, the bunchgrass was withered, the smoke of the pulp mill acrid in the wind from the west.

There were so many graves that I couln't find the ones I was looking for until I saw the clumsy figure of a stone angel, half life size, the face smiling idiotically, the fingers and tips of the wings broken. A single word, RYAN carved on the base of the statue, was hidden by tumbleweeds.

This, of course, must be Miss Stella' monument to her Dandy, no expense spared. Next to it, two flat slabs of granite marked her grave and Hogarth's. They all lay close at the end, as was fitting and proper. Even young David had the grace to keep silent while I stood with my own long thoughts that no boy could share.

Further up the hill I found the stones I had come to see, flat stones, side by side. Bending down, I pushed away the weeds and read the names of my uncle and aunt, faintly legible after the years of sun and snow.

But the earlier years were more vivid to me, more vivid than yesterday. The wars, the depressions, the fall of empires and the countless follies crammed into my lifetime were fading already to become unreal, wasted, absurd. And it was impossible, as I looked down on the flat stones, to explain, even to myself, why the forgotten townsfolk buried here now seemed greater, wiser, more successful than the famous personages I had known in the cities of the world.

Absurd, of course, and I didn't cry any more. I just looked across the bare, dusty hill and saw it again under snow and heard the tinkle of sleigh bells, the creak of harness, the snort of Tex's big Clydesdales, the thud of frozen earth on a wooden box. Who else remembered those times and the boy I had once been? Nobody. So I laid my bunch of roses on the stones and turned away.

David pointed to a gaunt, black horse nibbling the parched bunchgrass outside the fence, the first horse we'd seen in the Dry Belt.

"What's wrong with him?" David asked.

I saw then that the horse's spine drooped in the middle like a shallow letter U.

"He's a sway-back," I said. "Could have been born that way or ridden too young. It sometimes happens. But he's healthy."

David gazed at the sway-back and I could tell that he was thinking his own long thoughts. At last he said, "Gramp, were there cowboys and Indians in the olden days?"

"Sure, lots of them."

"Like the movies?"

"No, not like the movies. They were different, they were real."

"Wow! That must have been keen."

I looked down the hill on the new buildings and streets of Emerald Vale.

"Yes, keen," I said. "It was a wonderful little town, crazy but wonderful."